A10

- 4 FEB 2012

Drifter From Texas

The Cotton boys owned the town and nothing moved in or out without their say-so. Drifters weren't encouraged and the threat of lead in the air was usually enough to persuade them to move on. All except one: a dark-haired stranger who gave his name as Green.

When the Cottons tried to gun down an unarmed kid, Green took a hand against them. Now the Cotton boys were going to make an example of him to the rest of town. They didn't know what they were taking on, but would soon find out. . . .

Drifter From Texas

Frederick H. Christian

A Black Horse Western

ROBERT HALE · LONDON

ISBN 0 7090 7645 2

Robert Hale Limited
Clerkenwell House
Clerkenwell Green
London EC1R 0HT

Typeset by
Derek Doyle & Associates, Shaw Heath.
Printed and bound in Great Britain by
Antony Rowe Limited, Wiltshire

For Anthony Mock, Hornbold,
the delightful Mrs T.— and Mumbles.

CHAPTER ONE

'Are yu comin' out, or do I have to come in after yu?' The voice was immature, and broke in its highest register, but there was no gainsaying the deadly intent behind the words. They rang clear and sharp on the morning air. The speaker was a young man of perhaps twenty, with the clean and open face of a person who has never had a thing to hide. He was dressed in a worn, faded pair of Levi's, and a heavy work shirt; his boots were scuffed and worn.

The few pedestrians on the street at that hour had scattered fast as the boy had thundered up the street of Cottontown and swung down out of the saddle outside the town's only saloon – 'The Oasis' – to issue his challenge. They watched from behind windows or from the safety of doorways as he stood bareheaded in the dusty street, his eyes fixed on the batwing doors of the saloon, his right hand clenching and unclenching about the smooth butt of an old cap-and-ball Colt's Army model thrust into the waistband of his jeans.

'Buck Cotton! I'm countin' five!' the boy called. 'If yu ain't out here by then, I'm a-comin' in to get yu!'

The boy was oblivious to the owlish eyes of the spectators clustered at the windows of the saloon and, indeed, of every other building up and down the street.

'That's young Billy Hornby o' the Lazy H, ain't it?' queried one watcher. 'What's his quarrel with Buck Cotton?'

'Search me,' his neighbour replied, with bated breath. 'But he's shore loco to be pickin' it.'

The first speaker nodded. Crossing the Cottons was undoubtedly the unhealthiest pastime to pursue in this town.

This angry youth was apparently intent on bringing about his own destruction in the most reckless manner.

'One!' called Hornby. 'Two! Three! Four! Five!' His mouth set in a tight line. 'I'm comin' in for yu, Buck!'

The spectators by the windows flattened themselves against the walls of the saloon as the boy mounted the sidewalk and thrust his way through the batwing doors and into the saloon. There were no more than a dozen men in the place so early in the day. All of them turned to watch the reaction of the man at the far end of the long bar which ran the length of the saloon, object of the boy's heedless challenge.

This was a young man perhaps a year or two older than the boy who now stood glowering on the threshold of the saloon. Dressed in black, his clothes spotless, boots highly polished, Buck Cotton was almost a handsome man. His features were finely chiselled, and only the shifty eyes and a certain weakness about the mouth betrayed his basically shallow nature. Cotton's face was pale beneath his healthy tan, and his lower lip was clenched between his teeth to still its trembling. Desperately, his eyes shifted around the room for support or help, neither of which was forthcoming. The bystanders wanted no quarrel with this intruder with the blazing eyes. Buck Cotton's faltering gaze met that of his nemesis.

'I ain't fightin' yu, Hornby,' he whispered through dry lips. 'I got no quarrel with yu.'

'Yu sure as hell have,' grated the Lazy H man. 'Pull yore iron, yu sidewinder.'

The bartender, a tall, balding man with a lined, but kindly face, moved carefully along behind his bar towards young Hornby, keeping both hands well in sight on his spotless counter.

'Billy,' he remonstrated. 'Yu better cool off, son. This is big trouble. Climb on yore hoss an' skedaddle out o' here afore it gets wuss.'

'Keep tendin' yore bottles, Blass!' grated the kid. 'This is atween me an' that pizen toad over there.' He bent his narrowed gaze once more upon the cringing figure at the far end of the bar.

'Yu goin' to fight like a man or die like a dawg, Cotton?' he rasped. Buck Cotton lifted his hands away from his hips to an almost horizontal position, indicating his refusal to fight.

'I . . . I don't know what's eatin' yu, Billy,' he mumbled. 'I ain't about to draw on yu.' He turned his head towards the watching bystanders. 'Yo're all witnesses,' he croaked. 'I won't draw. My brothers. . . .'

'Damn yore brothers an' damn yu!' snapped Billy Hornby. He snatched the pistol from his waistband in a smooth sweep, and levelled it at Buck Cotton. Chairs scraped as men moved away from the line of fire, and the bartender ducked hastily down behind his bar.

'I reckon I'll have to put yu down like the dawg yu are, then,' Hornby went on, menacingly. 'At that, it'll be better'n yu deserve.'

His thumb eared back the spurred hammer of the old Colt. Buck Cotton cringed back against the bar, his hand held up in front of him, abject terror in every line of his body.

'Hold it right there, Hornby!'

The boy froze, the levelled gun needing only the relaxation of his thumb to send its deadly messenger on its errand.

'Uncork that cannon, boy! Slow an' easy!'

Every eye in the saloon except Hornby's had swivelled towards the speaker, a portly, grey-haired man with a tired, lined face who wore a silver star on his vest.

'Holy cow!' muttered one man watching this new development, 'I figgered Buck Cotton was a goner shore.'

'Ten seconds more an' he would'a' been,' grunted another. 'He's lucky Harry Parris was around.'

'Yeah, mighty handy, havin' yore own tame sheriff to bail yu out,' interposed a third, sardonically.

The sheriff moved crabwise across the room until he was in a position to cover both men. He gestured with his drawn gun.

'Let 'er drop, Billy,' he said, threateningly. 'I got yu dead to rights.'

For a moment, it looked as if young Hornby might dispute the command, and in the pregnant silence the sound of Parris's .45 being cocked made several men jump visibly.

Then, his shoulders slumping dejectedly, the boy complied. The gun clunked to the sawdusted wooden floor.

'Step away from it, Hornby,' commanded Parris. 'Easy, now.' Hornby took two steps backwards, so that he was no more than arm's length from the sheriff. As he did so, Buck Cotton scooped up the old revolver and in one movement had cocked and levelled it at Hornby's heart. Gone now was the look of abject fear, to be replaced by an expression of hate and triumph which distorted his handsome face, giving him the outward appearance of a devil incarnate.

'So. . . .' he snarled. 'Now, who're yu goin' to beef, tough boy?'

'I ought to've blown out yore light an' took a chance on yore mumblin' friend,' snapped Hornby. 'Yu ain't fit to live.'

'Watch yore lip, nester!' rapped Buck Cotton. 'Yu say too much an' I'll put yu down for good!'

'Take it easy, now, Buck,' interposed Parris. 'He ain't goin' no place. Yu, boy—' this to Hornby. 'What's all this about? Yu gone crazy tryin' to tree this town, assaultin' one o' our leadin' citizens?'

Scornfully Hornby jerked his head at Buck Cotton. 'Ask him,' he replied. 'He knows what it's about.'

Cotton looked momentarily uncomfortable, then a brazen expression settled itself upon his features.

'He's loco,' he told the sheriff. 'I don't know what he's talkin' about.'

'Yu better have some explanation, Hornby,' said Parris severely. 'Sim Cotton is goin' to want to know what yu took after his brother for.'

Hornby shrugged. It was as if he knew that nothing he said would make the slight difference, that no power on earth could alter the chain of events he had so impetuously set in motion. 'Yu reckon yore boss'll care whether I got a reason or not?' he asked the sheriff contemptuously.

'I'll thank yu to remember that Sim Cotton ain't my boss,' snapped Parris testily. 'I keep the law around here my way. Nobody else's.'

'Shore, Harry,' the boy said wearily. 'An' pigs have wings.'

'Watch yore lip, nester boy,' growled Buck Cotton. 'Yu ain't out o' the woods yet.'

'I'd say you'll be elderly afore yu get out o' where yu'll go for this,' Parris added. 'Assault with a deadly weapon. . . .'

Hornby looked at him, his eyes flat and expressionless.

'Get on with it, Parris,' he rapped. 'Don't bother tryin' to make it look good. Do what Sim Cotton pays yu for.'

Blass, the bartender, interposed at this point.

'Billy, don't talk like that,' he said. 'Yu'll get a trial. Won't he, Harry?'

'Shore he will,' said Parris. There was no inflexion in his voice.

'Yu can say yore piece then, boy,' the bartender continued. 'A jury. . . .'

'Jury! Cotton's handpicked verdict-makers! Yu know the ropes around here, Blass. The Cottons'll have me killed tryin' to escape like they've done with half a dozen oth—'

'Shut yore lyin' mouth!' As he screeched these words, Buck Cotton hurled an open-handed blow at Hornby, rocking him backwards and drawing a trickle of blood from a split lip. Hornby's muscular young frame tensed and almost automatically, the right hand drew back, bunched into a fist. In the same second, the old sheriff slid close in behind him, and he felt the uncompromising hardness of the gunbarrel in the small of his back. His hand fell to his side and as it did so, Cotton, his eyes gleaming now with hatred, once more rocked the prisoner's head with an open-handed slap

'Here now, wait a min—' began the bartender. He fell silent as Parris swung the sixgun barrel towards him.

'Stay out of this, Blass!' Parris warned.

Again Buck Cotton slapped the man in front of him.

'Tough as all get-out, ain't yu?' raged Buck Cotton. 'Big man! Yu an' that high an' mighty sister o' yores. Well, she ain't so high an' mighty any more, is she?'

He fell back as he uttered these words, for an ugly, almost insane growl of hatred was issuing from Billy Hornby's throat. All expression was gone from the boy's eyes, which held the same pale empty glare as those of a hunting puma. Without volition Hornby's hand reached forward for Buck Cotton's throat, the shoulder muscles stiff with killing rage.

'Yu . . . dirty . . .' Hornby took a step, two steps forward, his fingers clutching for this hated thing before him. In the same moment, Buck Cotton lurched backwards very rapidly, his eyes wide with ungoverned terror, pulling up the gun to ward off this nemesis, while Sheriff Parris, a cold smile on his mouth, cocked his pistol to blast Billy Hornby down from behind.

And in that moment, two shots rang out like thunder.

One of them rapped the old Colt's Army model out of Buck Cotton's hand and sent it hurtling across the bar, smashing into a bottle on the shelf there and yanking a curse from Buck's twisted mouth. The second, fired so close as to seem part of the first shot, zipped into the forearm muscles of the sheriff's right arm, knocking him spinning to the left, the cocked .45 exploding harmlessly into the air and leaving him reeling against the polished bar, struggling to turn and face this unexpected attack. Buck Cotton's hand flashed towards the holstered gun at his side as he too, wheeled around.

'Think about it for a moment,' was the sardonic warning. Though the words were quietly spoken, they conveyed a threat which the would-be killer dared not ignore.

'What the . . . who the hell are yu, mister?' Parris managed.

'I'm called Green,' was the monosyllabic reply. 'But don't bet on it.' Parris surveyed the speaker, who leaned against the wall of the saloon with the easy grace of the trained athlete, the smoke from a cigarette dangling in his mouth spiralling undisturbed towards the ceiling. Green looked like any other drifting cowpuncher. Still in his twenties, a slim-hipped, broad-shouldered *hombre* dressed in worn cowboy rig – blue shirt, silk bandanna, heavy leathern chaps, high-heeled boots – that was neat and serviceable. Only the twin gunbelts, the holsters tied down to his thighs with rawhide thongs, set him apart. There was a look about him. His lean, clean-shaven, deeply-bronzed face was saturnine, almost Indian except for the absence of the typical high cheekbones of the race. There was a difference too in the level eyes, as cold now as Polar seas, and in the quirk of humour which softened the hard lines of the mouth. Parris observed these details and drew a wrong conclusion.

'Stranger in town, doesn't know what he's gettin' into,' was his unspoken thought. He turned to the bartender.

'Blass, tell this jasper what he's pokin' his nose into'

'Trouble, I'll bet,' jeered Green. 'Allus been my downfall. Every time I see someone tryin' to gun down an unarmed man I go an' do it again. Keep still, yu!'

This snapped command froze Buck Cotton, whose hand had been stealthily easing towards his holstered gun.

'I ain't tellin' yu because yu deserve the warnin',' he told Cotton coldly. 'I just hate shootin' skunks out o' season.' His words brought the blood rushing to Buck Cotton's cheeks.

'Yu better be able to fight as good as yu can talk, mister,' he sneered. 'Yu don't know it yet, but yu just bought into more trouble than most men avoid in a lifetime.'

'There yu go again,' Green said mildly. 'Scarin' me to death. Yu'll have my knees knockin' if yu keep it up.' He addressed himself to young Hornby. 'Step away from them polecats, kid, and move over by the door.'

Hornby did as he was told, and then Green backed over until he stood alongside him.

Now that the imminent threat of death was seemingly past, Buck Cotton's confidence was returning. Parris, too, was struggling to put on a more dignified expression.

'Yu better head for the border, Green,' jibed Cotton. 'Yu stay in these parts an' yore life ain't worth a plugged nickel.'

'He's right, Mister Green,' whispered the boy. 'This is Sim Cotton's town. They catch us here an' we ain't got a prayer.'

Green nodded. 'Yore hoss outside?' Billy replied affirmatively. 'Then we better be moseyin'.' He turned to face the men in the saloon.

'I can usually hit what I shoot at,' he warned them. 'Don't go makin' the mistake o' stickin' yore head out o' the door for a few minnits if yu aim to keep it on yore neck.'

'Git while the goin's good, stranger,' screeched Buck Cotton. 'My brothers'll hunt yu down like dawgs.'

'That's about how I'd expect them to hunt,' grinned Green mirthlessly. He nodded to the boy and backed carefully towards the door. At that same moment, the head and shoulders of a very tall man appeared above the frame of the batwings. Green saw the expression on Sheriff Parris' face change, and wheeled to face this unseen threat but the man outside had already assessed the situation and was acting. His gunbarrel crashed down on Green's head, sending him stunned to the floor, and in a continuation of the movement, the man slashed sideways, catching Billy Hornby above the left ear, jarring the boy into insensibility. A second blow dropped Billy prostrate alongside his protector. Within another few minutes they were trussed like turkeys and dragged senseless by the heels across the street to the jail.

CHAPTER TWO

'If this is Paradise, I shore am disappointed.' Green's pained comment as he regained consciousness brought a wry smile to the bloodstained face of Billy Hornby. He surveyed his new-found friend and shook his head.

'Mister Green, yu look about the way I feel,' he vouchsafed. Indeed, both of them were sorry sights. Their clothes were dusty and stained, and the trickle of dried blood on Billy Hornby's forehead was matched by one which had oozed from the split in Green's scalp. Their hands and faces, too, were scratched from their unceremonious dragging across the wheel-rutted street of Cottontown.

'Looks like they drug us in here by the feet,' commented Green. He tested the ropes which bound his hands and feet. 'I shore am hawgtied.' There was no slack in his bonds; they had been expertly tied. 'This the jail?' he asked.

Hornby nodded, glancing gloomily about the tiny cell.

'Stands about opposite the saloon,' he told his companion. He hesitated for a moment. 'Mister Green . . . I never got a chance to thank yu for what yu done back there. . . .'

'Shucks, no call to,' interrupted Green. 'An' my friends call me Jim.' He looked keenly at the youngster for a moment, then asked a question.

'Buck is the younger brother out o' three,' Billy told him. 'The other two are Art an' Sim. Art's about yore age, I'd reckon, and Sim's the oldest. He's about thirty-five.'

'Then the town's named after their ol' man, I'm takin' it. He still around?'

Billy shook his head. 'Ol' Zeke died a few years back. He

15

settled this valley. Built the ol' Cottonwood ranch back in the hills north o' town after he came back from the War. There used to be an old Army post about fifty miles south o' town – Fort Lane. Zeke was a good businessman. Figgered the Army boys needed a place they could relax in, take a smile when they wanted to. He built a store, an' a saloon, about halfway between his ranch an' the Fort. Brung some o' his relations in from Texas to run 'em. Town just growed up around them. Natural enough, they called it Cottontown.'

Green nodded his understanding. Many a man had grown rich and fat on Army custom.

'I expect he was supplyin' the Fort with beef an' horses, too?' he hazarded.

'Yu bet he did,' Billy replied. 'He had all the contracts sewed up. Nobody else in these parts could get a look-in. An' then the Army pulled out.'

'When was that?' asked the tall puncher.

'About '73, durin' the depression. Fort's ruined now. A few Mex sheepherders live there. Ain't another settlement within a hundred miles, an' this valley bein' a sort o' bowl, Cottontown keeps it alive. Folk who live in these parts toe the line the Cottons draw, or git. When ol' Zeke died, Sim took over. It's his town now. What he says goes. The Cottons do what they like. Any arguments, an'—' He drew a forefinger across his throat.

'An' yu . . . ?' prompted Green.

'I run a small place south o' town – the Lazy H. My old man ran it until he died – that was the same year ol' Zeke Cotton cashed in his chips. I been tryin' to make the place pay ever since, but it ain't easy.'

'Where's the market for yore beef?'

'Silver City,' Billy told him. 'But we ain't allowed to sell independent. The Cottons sell all the beef out o' this valley. We got to drive our cattle on to Cottonwood range, an' they pay their price for beef. Then they pool the herd an' sell down in Silver City.'

'Yu mean they fix the prices, an' yu can't kick? Ain't anyone tried to drive his own herd to Silver City?'

'Shore, one or two o' the local men tried it,' continued Billy. 'They was either hit by raiders in the night an' had their herds run off, or they was ambushed. One man – old vinegary gent by the name o' Bert Williams, swore nobody was goin' to tell him how much he could sell his beef for – got burned down from behind. That put an end to it. Nobody needed it spellin' out. From then on, everyone sold their beef to the Cottons, allasame good boys.'

'The Cottons never had any trouble on the trail, I'm takin' it?'

'They claim nobody'd dare hit an outfit o' their size. No, they ain't never been touched.'

Green pondered for a moment, his lips pursed. He shifted on the rude bunk bed into a more comfortable position, easing his cramped arms and legs.

'These ropes musta bin tied by an Injun,' he complained. Though he felt easier, his body was one big ache.

'So the Cottons git yu both ways,' he proposed. 'They cut yu to the bone on yore cattle prices, an' then hold yu up on prices o' supplies. Right?'

'Right!' nodded Billy grimly. 'Anyone squawks, an' he winds up in an alley with his head broke.'

Green's mind was busy. The pattern of the Cottons' power was not at all unfamiliar. A similar set of circumstances had obtained in many of the unsettled areas of the West – in Lincoln County they had brought about range war when the people rebelled. 'Ain't the townsfolk ever shown any opposition, or any o' the smaller ranchers?' he asked.

'Once,' Billy told him, his voice unemotional. 'Few years back, just after Zeke Cotton died, the town doctor, Dave Hight, tried to get a Townspeople's Committee together. One mornin' he was found behind the livery stable, about ten yards from his own back door, beaten within an inch o' his life, an' one o' his legs broke. He ain't never walked right since. They found a piece o' paper pinned on his shirt. It just said "Be warned!" Ever since then, the Cottons have had this town buttoned up.' Green shook his head. 'Shore sound like a mean bunch!' he opined.

'There's a few folk ain't scared to speak their minds – up to a point,' Billy informed him. 'But yu got to walk pretty wary.'

'Which is a sight more'n yu did,' grinned Green. 'Yu want to tell me what it was I got myself into?'

Billy's young face set into hard lines. 'I'd as lief not talk about it, Jim.' Then his expression softened an iota. 'Still . . . I reckon yu got a right to know. I got home from checkin' the range this mornin'. I found my sister – she's eighteen, Jim, eighteen years old – lyin' in the house, on the floor. Her clothes was in tatters. She was sobbin' like a 'pache squaw. . . .' His voice broke, and he struggled briefly, ineffectually, against his bonds, as if his very rage would burst them. Green managed to find somewhere else to look while the boy fought for control. 'She was pretty bad scared but she hadn't been . . . hurt. Told me that Buck Cotton had come to the house. Didn't want to tell me more – she knowed what I'd do. She said he had been waitin' until I was gone afore he come a-visitin'. Then he just. . . .' A shudder of suppressed anger shook his shoulders.

'I took her down to the ol' Fort an' got a Mex woman to look after her. Then I lit out like a bat out o' hell for town. Sent Doc Hight out there, an' then I went lookin' for Buck Cotton. Yu know the rest.'

Green bowed his head. The boy's unreasoning anger had precipitated a smouldering confrontation. 'Gonna be inter-estin' to see what these Cotton jaspers dream up for us,' he told himself. He watched the youngster as an expression of disgust crossed Billy's face.

'I oughta've killed him when I had the chance!' spat the boy.

'Been a pretty empty gesture if yu'd got killed doin' it, wouldn't it?' was Green's reasonable reply. 'That Parris was shore achin' to put a slug atween yore shoulder blades.' Changing the subject he asked Billy who would look after his sister.

'I reckon Doc Hight'll take care o' Jenny,' Billy told him. 'I'd guess them two is goin' to get married afore long. They shore get all moony-eyed when they're settin' on our front

18

porch.' This with the typical disgust of the young man for such 'romantic foofarraw'. Green smiled to himself.

'This Doc Hight sounds like a good man. Any others in town we can hope for a square deal from?'

Billy's expression was glum. 'Not many,' he admitted. 'The barkeep, Blass, is a fair man, but he works for the Cottons. They own the Oasis. Mebbe Bob Davis who runs the general store an' one or two o' the men on the smaller spreads south o' town. That's about all. This is Cottontown, Jim. I shore am sorry I got yu into this.'

Green did not reply. He was busily inspecting their cell more closely and was not inspired to hope by what he saw. The tiny room was no more than six feet square. Straw covered the tamped dirt floor, and a tiny barred window set in one wall about seven feet from the ground let in light and air. The door looked like solid oak, and was studded with iron bolts. There was no Judas window, nor any kind of break in its surface. The walls of the cell were of adobe, the universal building bricks of the Southwest, and he guessed that they would be at least three feet thick.

'Not a hope o' breakin' out,' he muttered. 'Even if our hands was free – which same they ain't.'

Billy watched his friend's careful inspection of the cell wordlessly. When Green was finished he said:

'I could'a' told yu not to bother, but I didn't figger yu'd take any notice, anyway.'

Green smiled. 'Allus like to look for myself. Just to be shore.'

'What I said,' replied his cell mate. 'The on'y place built stronger than the jail is the Bank.'

Before Green could comment further, they heard heavy footsteps in the corridor outside their cell, and the jangling of keys, followed by the grating metallic sound of a heavy bolt being pulled back.

The door swung outwards to reveal Sheriff Parris, hands on hips, regarding his two prisoners with a self-satisfied smile. Behind him stood two heavily-built men, both armed with shotguns.

'Well, well, if it ain't the remains of the Rebel Army,' he gloated. 'Yu boys look like somethin' fell on yore heads.' He turned to the man on his left. 'Cut their feet loose, an' mind how yu do it! Yu two jaspers – take it slow an' easy! Jackson, here, is a nervous sort o' feller, an' yu don't want his finger twitchin'. These walls take a lot o' scrubbin' if one o' them cannons goes off.' This macabre reference to their fate in the event of any show of resistance was not lost on the two prisoners.

After their feet had been freed, and they had stamped around for a moment to get the circulation moving again, Green asked a question.

'Where are yu goin'?' Parris laughed, a hearty, evil laugh. 'Why yo're not bein' kept waitin' around, wonderin' what's to happen. We're takin' yu over to the saloon, an' yo're goin' to be tried.'

'Tried?' cried Billy Hornby. 'Tried for what?'

Parris grinned, his tobacco-stained teeth glinting crookedly beneath his grizzled moustache. He held up a hand and ticked off the charges on his fingers.

'Obstructin' an officer in the course o' his duty, assault with a deadly weapon, breach o' the peace, firin' a gun inside town limits, felonious woundin' of an officer o' the law, incitin' a riot, attempted murder, vagrancy – hell, take yore pick. We got enough to hang yu two *hombres* higher'n Haman!'

CHAPTER THREE

'Hang!'

Although Green was bound, and covered by two men with the lethal power of twin-barrelled shotguns ready to blast the man down at the slightest sign of trouble, Parris scuttled backwards at the cold deadliness in Green's voice.

'Watch him!' he squeaked.

'Yu better, yu misfit!' snapped Green. 'What kind o' law d'yu have in these parts, anyway?' Parris's smile was evil incarnate, and the two burly deputies behind him exchanged indulgent smiles at what seemed to be Green's naïveté.

'Yu'll find out what kind,' gloated Parris, 'any minnit now. March, damn yu!'

The taller of the two deputies gestured imperiously with the shotgun, and the two prisoners were shepherded into the outer office, and thence into the bright morning sunlight of the crowded street. As they walked across its dusty width, Green noticed the small crowd of onlookers watching from the porch of the Oasis break, its members scuttling inside the saloon to gain vantage points from which to watch the forthcoming trial. The saloon was filling rapidly when they entered it, and a hum of conversation arose as they marched up the gangway between the rows of chairs set out for the citizens to watch. Between thirty and forty men were congregated in the saloon, sitting or lounging on benches which had been set along the walls. The tables had been moved to one side, and an open space had been left at the far end of the saloon, in which was placed a table and chair. The front row of seats had been kept vacant, and it was to these that the prisoners were led. Green and the boy sat with one of the deputies on either side of them. Parris took the gangway seat.

The onlookers, several of whom had been witness to the events earlier in the day, filled the air with speculation and gossip about the saturnine stranger, sitting now as if unconcerned by his predicament, who had so unexpectedly intervened in the fight between Billy Hornby and Buck Cotton.

'All rise!' Parris' bawling voice cut across the layers of muted conversation, stilling them. Every man in the room got to his feet at the sheriff's command, while the two prisoners were yanked rudely upright. Green turned his head to see the batwing doors swinging behind the passage of a small, thickset old man in a suit which looked as though he hadn't taken it off for a year. Stained and disreputable, his appearance was hardly improved by the unshaven stubble, filthy linen, and rheumy, bloodshot eyes of the confirmed drinker. A wag in the crowd called out 'How about a quick one, judge?' and was rewarded by an evil glare from the shuffling old man, and a malevolent, warning glance from the deputy on Green's right.

Now, however, all eyes swung back to the doorway and the old man was temporarily forgotten as two big men shouldered their way into the saloon. There was a murmur from the crowd, and Green heard one man remark 'It figgered Sim an' Art would ride in.' So these were the Cottons! He examined them covertly from beneath lowered brows, pretending to be busy rolling a cigarette.

Art Cotton was tall and slim. His dark hair was cut short, and he was almost a handsome man. Only the slight twist of his lips, and a jagged knife scar marring the right cheek, white against the tan, marred the face, giving it an almost permanent sneer. The cold, flat, expressionless eyes, however, spoke of the killer slumbering beneath the seemingly good-looking exterior. Art Cotton was dressed in range garb, and a heavy revolver hung at his right hip.

It was his older brother, however, who caught the attention and held it. A huge man, easily six feet tall, and as broad across the shoulders as a bull, Sim Cotton looked like a man accustomed to obedience and power. Age had thickened his middle, and his hair was iron grey, beneath the expensive sombrero. His grizzled bushy eyebrows almost concealed slate-coloured eyes, small and set close together to give the heavy features an air of piggish cunning. Despite a film of dust, his heavy broadcloth suit was obviously of good material, and across his ample belly looped a heavy silver watch chain. He stalked down the gangway like a bear, not deigning to look at the two prisoners. Neither did he even nod to the men who hastily vacated their seats in the front row on the opposite side of the gangway to where Hornby and Green stood. Both men sat down heavily and Sim Cotton nodded shortly to the old man who had preceded them into the saloon. Green's keen gaze remained on the doorway. Behind the Cottons a very tall man, standing head and shoulders above anyone else in the place, had moved quietly into the room. This man's long face was watchful and composed, and the cold blue eyes moved constantly around the room. The man's hair was long, hanging low on the collar of his blue denim shirt. He had a broken nose. Green nudged Billy, and pointing with his chin, looked his inquiry at the boy.

'Cottons' top gun,' muttered the boy. 'Name o' Chris Helm.' For the first time, then, Green noted the fancy 'Texan rig' two-holster belt, the heavy guns nestling in the oiled leather, the tips of the holsters secured to the thighs with thongs decorated with Mexican dollars beaten flat.

'Fancy guns,' he told himself, 'but dangerous – an' fast, I'd reckon.' He had the feeling he had seen Helm somewhere before, and sat pondering this.

'Court's in session,' rasped the old man at the table, regaining the attention of the crowd. Green sardonically noted the palsied twitching of the liver-spotted hands, the constant furtive licking of dry lips.

'Looks like a jasper who never takes a drink when he's sleepin',' he muttered sardonically to the boy. Billy nodded, and was about to reply, when the guard next to him jabbed him wickedly in the ribs with his shotgun. The boy lapsed into silence, but his eyes confirmed Green's estimation of the man at the table.

Harry Parris got to his feet, and lumbered forward to stand before the table.

'Judge Martin Kilpatrick's presidin' over thisyere court,' he told the crowd. 'Keep quiet back there! Norris, bring the first prisoner forward.'

There was a stir of anticipation among the spectators as Green was herded to stand before the table. He turned to see Sim Cotton's piggy eyes weighing him the way a cattleman judges the weight of a steer. Judge Kilpatrick peered at Green.

'Your name,' he snapped.

'James Green.'

'Your occupation?'

'Cowhand.'

'Where do you hail from, Green?'

'Texas, originally. I been workin' down Tucson way.'

'And what is your business in Cottontown?'

'No business. Just passin' through,' Green told him.

Kilpatrick looked towards the sheriff.

'What charges are you bringing, Harry?'

Parris faced the crowd, inflating his chest and stating pompously, 'Assault with a deadly weapon, obstructin' an officer in the course o' his duty – namely, me – an' firin' a pistol inside the town limits. Also incitin' a riot, deliberate woundin', an' a couple o' other misdemeanours we ain't aimin' to bother yu with.'

There was nervous laughter from the watching audience, and Green noted that most of them were watching Sim Cotton's face. Cotton deigned to smile slowly, and the laughter became more general. When Cotton's smile faded, the laughter stopped.

'Order!' Kilpatrick banged on the table with a wooden gavel. He then asked 'Were there any witnesses to this?'

'About twenty people seen it, Martin. I can call 'em if yu wish . . . ?' He asked this question facing Sim Cotton. Green saw Cotton shake his head imperceptibly, and was not surprised to hear the old man mumble 'That won't be necessary, Harry. Court will accept your word.' He pondered for a moment. 'Have you any means, Green?'

'Money, yu mean? I had about fifty-eight dollars when I was thrown in yore calaboose. I ain't got it now,' Green told him. Kilpatrick looked inquiringly at Parris, and the sheriff nodded.

'When we disarmed the prisoners, we took all their belongin's off them,' he told the old man. 'Green here had the money he sez, an' not much else. No letters, no identification. Two guns, he was wearin'. They look like they been well cared for,' he added darkly. Kilpatrick's eyes met those of the puncher, and for a brief moment, Green saw the spark of malignancy behind them, 'You are accused on four counts, Green, all of them serious charges. You're a stranger, without means of identification, and precious little money. A drifter, a saddle tramp. We don't need that kind in Cottontown. Four charges – you heard what the sheriff said. How do you plead: guilty or not guilty?'

'Yu mean it makes a difference?' was Green's sardonic response. He raised his eyebrows and looked surprised, and his byplay was greeted by a slight snicker from somewhere in the audience. Sim Cotton turned and glared at the onlookers.

'Your humour is about as well-judged as your actions,' rapped the old man at the table. 'Have you anything further to say?'

'I got plenty to say!' snapped the cowboy. 'To begin with, I just managed to stop yore sheriff an' that young sidewinder over yonder—' he gestured contemptuously towards Buck Cotton, who sat glowering on one of the benches alongside the saloon wall – 'from tryin' to salivate an unarmed man. What did yu expect me to do – sit an' watch while they blew his light out?'

'The sheriff was apprehending a criminal, Green. Your statement does not alter the charges against you. Did you assault the sheriff?'

'If you mean did I stop him from killin' the kid, yes—'

'And did you fire your gun?' droned Kilpatrick inexorably.

'Shore I did. I was—'

'Did you then rearm a disarmed prisoner?'

Green shrugged. 'For an impartial judge, yu shore seem to know a hell of a lot about what happened,' he said. 'Yu ain't heard any fac's but yu got yore mind made up for yu already Get on with it, yu ol' fraud.'

A mottled flush rose in Kilpatrick's face, staining his wattled neck. He banged on the table.

'Be silent!' he screeched. 'You are in contempt of court!'

'Yo're right, on'y I ain't shore the word contempt is strong enough,' came the reply from the unperturbed Green. Once again, as he spoke, he caught a signal passing from Sim Cotton to the judge. Kilpatrick leaned back in his seat, mopping his face with a filthy red handkerchief.

'Court finds the charges proved. You are guilty on all counts, Green. Fined fifty-eight dollars and to be taken beyond the city limits, and there turned loose. I don't think this town wants to even feed scum like you,' he hissed venomously.

The ruthless effrontery of the old man's actions, and this farce of a trial, a travesty of every judicial procedure, took away Green's breath. Then he spoke.

'Well, if that's yore idea of law, this town'd be better off with a horned toad for a judge.'

A movement caught Green's eye, and he turned to see Sim Cotton lumbering towards him.

'Yo're pretty cocky, son,' was the soft-spoken remark which opened the exchange. 'Don't push yore luck too far. This town won't stand for it.'

'This town'd stand for bein' boiled down for tallow if yu said the word, wouldn't it, Cotton?' Green's eyes locked with the older man's, and it was Cotton's slatey gaze which dropped first.

'I'm bein' as fair with yu as any man,' Cotton told him. 'Yo're gettin' off light. But don't make the mistake o' comin' back to Cottontown – ever.' There was no emphasis in the words, but the threat was plain and lay between the two men like a knife. Sim Cotton turned abruptly, dismissing Green from his reckoning. Norris, the tall deputy who had been guarding Green earlier, gestured at the seat Green had formerly occupied, emphasising the unspoken command with the simultaneous movement of the shotgun.

Green shrugged and sat down. One movement in resistance and he could be shot down like a dog without a hand being lifted by these men watching. His lip curled; he surveyed the inhabitants of Cottontown with contempt. They, however, were quite unconscious of his vitriolic gaze. Their attention now was completely focused upon the sturdy back of Billy Hornby, who had been hustled to his feet and was standing, as his fellow-prisoner had stood, before the table.

'Your name?' Kilpatrick began his questioning.

'Yu know my name, Kilpatrick,' Billy said, shortly. 'An' yu

know my occupation an' where I live an' yu know I ain't a drifter an' yu know I ain't broke.'

'Not yet yu ain't,' murmured someone behind Green, and the words struck a chill in him. These people were like the ancient Romans he had read about somewhere, waiting avidly for someone to be torn to pieces by wild animals – and enjoying the waiting.

'Answer the questions, yu!' Harry Parris bustled forward, gun in hand. 'An' don't give His Honour no lip, if yu know what's good for yu!'

'Sit down, Harry!'

Sim Cotton's deep voice crackled like a whiplash, and Parris, starting as though he had been stung, took a step backwards, tangling his own feet, and stumbling on to the knees of his deputy. Laughter sprang to the throats of the watchers, and again died stillborn when it was seen that the Cottons were not laughing. Green kept his eyes fixed now on Art Cotton, for he had noticed that the man was completely ignoring the proceedings in the crowded room. Art Cotton sat, his long, white hands dangling limply between his legs, his expressionless eyes fixed unseeingly upon the blank wall in front of him, looking neither right nor left.

'That one's a renegade or my name's Shaughnessy,' Green told himself. Meanwhile, the judge had listened to Billy's self identification and now asked Parris to state the charges against the boy.

'There's plenty o' charges, Judge,' Parris said, pompously, 'but the main one'll do to tie to – attempted murder!'

A whisper of conversation grew among the spectators, those who had not yet heard the story of the fight in the saloon hearing it now from others who had either witnessed it or been told about it. The old man banged once more upon the table until silence fell.

'That's better,' he nodded. 'Now, Hornby. You plead guilty or not guilty?'

'Not guilty!' Billy's voice was clear, his head held proud and high.

'I see. Do you wish to be tried by jury?'

Billy shrugged. 'Why not? Give these animals their fun.'

'That will do,' snapped Kilpatrick, like a schoolteacher. 'You will receive a fair trial in this court.'

'Yu won't mind if I don't hold my breath waitin'?'

Kilpatrick's face mottled again. 'You are in contempt,' he screeched. 'I will not permit this kind of insult to the dignity of the court!'

Sim Cotton nodded, and again raised his voice slightly.

'Yu, boy. Don't let yore tongue run away with yu.'

'Why?' snapped Billy, defiantly. 'What difference does it make?'

'Yu might have to pay a big fine,' Cotton pointed out, his voice still level. 'An' since yu ain't got any money, mebbe the court would have to confiscate anythin' yu own – like yore ranch, mebbe.' Billy's face fell, and the anger receded from his expression to be replaced by frustration and shame. Cotton's well-aimed verbal barb had now robbed him of even the defence of bitter jibes. He could not afford to jeopardise all he owned for the sake of a brief gratification.

'Well, boy, speak!' rattled Kilpatrick. 'Do you want trial by jury?'

Billy nodded wordlessly, and Kilpatrick, after a brief glance at Sim Cotton for confirmation, inclined his head towards Sheriff Parris.

'Empanel a jury, Sheriff,' he told the lawman.

'I already got that done, Judge,' interposed Parris, holding up a hand and waving it airily towards a group of men bunched together at the side of the room alongside Buck Cotton. 'I figgered that Hornby'd ask for jury trial, and I picked some o' the boys out in advance to save time.' He turned towards the group, and told them: 'Yu boys take up yore seats an' line 'em up alongside the judge, there. Make it lively, now.'

Green watched Billy Hornby's face become even more bitter as he saw the jury of his 'peers' chosen by the cunning Parris. Drunks, bar-scourings, and minor hangers-on of the Cotton clan – what hope had he from such as these? Billy Hornby shook his head. There was nothing he could do. There were several men he failed to recognise, tough-looking fellows whose presence he did not fully comprehend until he saw the leering countenance of Buck Cotton; no doubt the youngest of the Cotton brood had recruited these men himself to make double sure of the verdict.

'Sheriff, outline the circumstances of the case for the jury,' the judge bid Parris. Nothing loath, Parris strutted into the space in front of the two Cotton brothers.

'This one –' he jerked his thumb at Billy, '– rode into town this mornin' about ten. He stood outside the saloon an' yelled that he was comin' in to kill young Buck Cotton, there. Didn't say why. Buck remained in the saloon. Refused to brawl in the streets. Sent a man to get me. I was in my office, an' got over to the Oasis just as fast as I could. Got there in time to see that one' – he jerked his head again towards Billy, '– threatenin' Buck Cotton with a pistol. Buck warn't even armed. . . .'

'That's a lie!' burst out Billy. 'He was heeled.'

'Have you a witness to this fact?' interposed Kilpatrick.

'Shore I have! Green there seen it, didn't you, Jim?

Green nodded. 'Cotton was wearin' a gun,' he said flatly.

Kilpatrick regarded him sourly, then turned to face Buck Cotton.

'Bucky, were you armed?'

Young Cotton uncoiled his length lazily, and got to his feet, an arrogant smirk on his face.

'Nope, I wasn't, Uncle Martin. I mean Judge.'

There was a murmur of amusement, quickly stilled by Kilpatrick's gavel. The old man turned in his chair to face the jury.

'The jury will take due note that the accusation of the prisoner is substantiated only by a convicted criminal, a proven troublemaker, while it is denied by the brother of our leading family.'

He smiled at Sim Cotton, who nodded portentously.

'The jury will know whom to believe, I am sure,' he added. The twelve men nodded, almost in unison.

'Carry on, Harry,' the judge told the sheriff.

Parris again resumed his actorish stance.

'When Buck, there, didn't choose to brawl with this young feller, he got real mad. Had blood in his eye for shore. Claimed he was goin' to shoot Buck down where he stood – an' he still hadn't give no reason for his quarrel. That was when I stepped in an' got the drop on him.'

He looked around proudly, as if expecting applause.

'Do you deny any of this, Hornby?' Kilpatrick's face was wooden.

'The fac's are in there someplace,' retorted Billy. 'But yu'd have to be smarter than yu look to find 'em.'

'Be assured we shall,' was the icy jibe. 'Continue, Sheriff.'

'At this point,' continued Parris, 'just as I'm about to march Hornby off to the hoosegow, this other jasper, Green, puts in his oar. He takes two shots at me, one o' which goes wild, an' the other hittin' me in the arm.' He rolled back his shirt sleeve to reveal the grimy, bloodstained bandage on his forearm. 'A lucky shot I reckon, but it knocked me off my balance an' made me drop my gun. Whereupon this feller Green pulls Hornby aside, an' is all set to run for it when Chris Helm, who's in town an' has heard the shootin', arrives at the door behind the two prisoners. He sees what's up in a flash, an' buffaloes the both of them. We drug 'em over to the jail, an' that was that.'

'You say that the prisoner here intended to kill Buck Cotton?' asked Kilpatrick.

'He was shoutin' it all over town, Martin,' replied the sheriff. 'I can produce a dozen witnesses—'

'No need, no need,' Kilpatrick waved an airy hand. 'Nobody doubts your veracity, Harry.' He turned to the jury again. 'Did any of you men see or hear Hornby threatening to kill Buck Cotton?' Several of the jurymen nodded. One of them stood up, a roughly dressed man with a broken nose. 'I shore as hell did, Judge,' he called. Kilpatrick nodded, as if these words were all the proof that was needed.

'It would seem to be an open and shut case. The accused was heard to threaten the life of an unarmed man. He threatened him with a gun, and was heard to say that he would kill him. Only the timely intervention of the sheriff prevented murder. As it was, shots were fired; the sheriff was wounded.' He turned towards Billy, frowning. 'I will ask the jury for its verdict unless you have something to say, prisoner. I warn you, however, that it had better not be anything insulting to this court.'

'I misdoubt I could think of anything which would insult

this court,' was Billy's cold reply, but his irony was completely lost upon the elephant hide of the old judge who was leaning back in his chair, confident that his task was completed. But Billy was not finished. 'If I was out o' here, I'd take after that polecat again!' Kilpatrick leaned forward sharply.

'Then perhaps we shall have to ensure that you are prevented from doing so, won't we?' There was malignant evil lurking deep in his reddened eyes, and a message passed between him and the older Cotton, unspoken but explicit.

'Jury, have you heard enough?'

The broken-nosed man who had spoken earlier stood up.

'We shore have, Judge. We don't need to waste any more time considerin' any verdict. That young hellion's guilty as hell!' Billy's lips tightened at these words, but he made no other motion. An excited buzz of conversation swept through the room now, and the spectators craned to get a better view of the condemned man. Kilpatrick cleared his throat, and banged upon the table for silence.

'Hornby, you've been found guilty. It now becomes my painful duty to pronounce sentence on you.'

A hush descended upon the listening audience. For the first time, Art Cotton leaned forward, his flat eyes watching the proceedings with something like interest. His brother leaned back in his chair, arms spread wide along the backs of his own and his brother's seats, his legs crossed; a long cigar in his thick lips. He looked as if he was enjoying himself in his own parlour.

'The sentence of the court is that you be taken to the Territorial prison, by the sheriff of this town, and delivered there to serve a sentence of ten years hard labour for the wilful and deliberate attempt at assassination you have perpetrated today. Sheriff, see to it that my sentence is carried out!' He banged once upon the table with his hammer and stood up. With a last baleful glance at his victim, he shuffled off down to the other end of the room, where the bartender had set up a bottle of whiskey and a glass. Kilpatrick gulped a large dose down like water, and splashed another into the glass in the time it took Parris and his deputies to prod Green to his feet and precede Billy through the jeering crowd of spectators out into the street

31

and towards the jail. As they crossed the street, Green heard Sim Cotton's bull voice shouting 'Set 'em up for everyone, Blass!' and heard the ragged cheer which followed this command.

'That'll make him popular,' commented Billy bitterly. 'In a few hours they'll be thankin' him for treatin' them like dawgs.'

'Yu shut yore yap, Hornby!' snapped Parris. 'No more talkin'.'

'I'll talk when I please, yu fat tub o' lard,' retorted Billy. 'I ain't takin' orders from yu, an' that's whatever.'

'Yu'll take 'em when we step out for Santa Fe,' Parris reminded him. They clumped into the little office, and the deputy called Norris motioned Green to sit down. Billy was shoved through the heavy door leading into the corridor where the cells lay, and in a moment the puncher heard the heavy door bang shut, and the grating sound of the metal bold being shot. Parris and his other deputy came back into the office.

'Yo're movin' on, Green,' the sheriff told the puncher levelly. 'An' yu better keep on movin' if yu've got the sense God gave ants. Yu show yore head in this town again an' someone'll shoot it off. Dan!' This to the shorter of the two deputies. 'Yu an' Jerry ride a ways with Mr Green here. Make shore he takes the right road.'

He looked meaningfully at the deputy, who nodded.

'I got yu, Harry,' he said 'We'll take care of it.'

Green had not missed the inflexions in their voices, and he recalled what Billy had told him in the jail.

'Can I see the kid afore I go?' he asked.

'Yu can talk to him through the door,' Parris allowed. 'One minute. Go with him, Dan. An' keep him covered the whole time.'

Green stood up and preceded the deputy into the dark, cool corridor. He stopped outside the heavy door. It was closed by two heavy metal bolts, one at the top and one at the bottom. There was no padlock.

'Billy!' he called. 'Yu hear me?'

'I hear yu, Jim,' came the boy's voice, muffled by the thickness of the cell door. 'Yu watch out. Remember what I told yu.'

'Keep yore chin up,' Green shouted. 'Don't quit yet.'

'I ain't about to. Watch yoreself, Jim.'

'Yu, too, kid.'

'Come on, that's a plenty,' growled Dan. 'Yu had yore minnit.'

He hustled Green back into the outer office. Parris looked up expectantly. 'What did they say?' he asked cunningly.

Dan reported the conversation, and Parris nodded.

'I thought yu might have some idea o' comin' back to help the kid,' he said, peering at Green shrewdly.

'Hell, ain't nothin' I could do now,' Green said, a bland look on his face. 'I'm shore regrettin' I ever came near this place.'

'Now yo're thinkin' straight,' Parris told him. 'Get goin', boys.'

'Don't I get my guns back?' asked the puncher.

'Where yo're headin' yu won't be need yore guns,' was the chilling reply. 'Besides, we don't want yu changin' yore mind, do we?' He grinned evilly. 'Dan, Jerry, get this saddletramp out o' here. I got work to do.'

The deputy called Jerry grabbed Green's arms and hustled him out into the street. The two men helped the bound puncher on to his horse and motioned him to lead the way up the street, almost completely deserted except for a few loungers on the porch of the saloon who watched incuriously as the three man procession headed out of the town. They headed south, across the wooden bridge which spanned the Bonito, and out into the rolling, gully-creased foothills which lay to the south of Cottontown. Once they were clear of the town, the two deputies, their shotguns cradled in their arms, lagged about three yards behind Green, keeping their distance constant, never coming near enough for him to make any move against them, never falling behind sufficiently to allow him to contemplate making a dash for freedom. The skin on Green's back crawled. He knew the old Mexican *ley del fuego* – the unwritten law under which prisoners were shot down 'trying to escape' in order to relieve their captors of the necessity of guarding them. When a man was wanted dead or alive the easiest way to bring him in was across a saddle. The infamous bounty hunters had made this law their own, covering their foul actions with the thin coating of legality.

'Shore wouldn't pay to make a run for it,' he told himself. 'That's just what they'd like me to do. But if I don't, I'm a goner anyway.' They descended a narrow defile, the weather-scoured rock walls of which were bare, relieved only in a few places by scattered clumps of brush clinging precariously where an earth-filled crevice afforded root-hold, huge rocks and thickets of prickly pear making detours inevitable and progress slow.

From time to time, as they rode along, Green tested his bonds, but they had been expertly tied. Indeed, he reflected, his silent guards were just as professional. Not once had either of them spoken, and yet their moves were as if planned. Neither of them had once come within striking distance, yet neither had ever been more than a few yards away from the prisoner at any time.

'Probably done this enough times to have it off pat,' he reflected grimly. He glanced at the sun. One o'clock or there-abouts. Sooner or later they were going to act. How would it come? A blasting sound, a tearing pain, blackness? No warning of the fatal moment, or the perhaps worse experience of facing the two men and waiting those eternal seconds as their fingers tightened on the triggers? Despite the heat of the sun a chill entered his veins. How far had they come? Five miles, seven maybe. Despite his iron control, Green felt an instinctive desire to break the menacing nerve-shattering silence.

'Shore could do with a drink,' he said aloud.

'Yu'll get one when we're ready,' Norris told him from behind. 'Keep movin', cowboy.'

The stillness of the wide open country wrapped around them again like a shroud. The blazing sun hung in a dome of cloudless blue. Nothing moved. No bird, no lizard darting among the rocks, nothing – Nature seemed to have deserted this desolation, leaving a silence like that of the tomb. They rode in this silence for perhaps another mile. Then the one called Dan said:

'This'll do. Get down, Green.'

CHAPTER FOUR

'Yu stupid fool!'

The flat, sharp sound of an open-handed slap echoed around the spare room of the house owned by Fred Mott, Sim Cotton's cousin, the town banker. It was a small room, containing only a table with an oil lamp, a few chairs, a bunk and a roll top desk. Mott, a thin, balding, bespectacled man, used it for a 'study', but whenever Sim Cotton needed a bed in town, he utilised this room, snoring on the rough bunk which filled one wall.

It was against this now that Buck Cotton sprawled, a trickle of blood emerging from the split lip caused by his older brother's contemptuous blow.

'But Sim . . .' he began.

' "But Sim!" ' mimicked the bigger man in a squeaking voice. ' "It was all in fun, Sim." You thick-headed oaf! How many times've I told yu to steer clear o' them nesters? How many times? Tell me, yu pup!'

'Yu've told me plenty o' times, Sim,' confessed Buck Cotton, miserably.

'Yet yu still go an' raise a ruckus with one o' their women,' was the biting retort. 'I reckon Pa forgot to send for brains when yu was born.'

He turned to Art Cotton, who was sitting straddling a chair, his arms folded along its back, watching the scene with impassive eyes.

'What did the doctor say, Art?'

Art Cotton shrugged.

'Said the gal'd had a shock. Nothin' serious wrong with her.

He'd love to've spit in my eye. Think he's smitten himself. Yu shore picked a wrong 'un there, Bucky. Next time, yu'd better go down to the ol' Fort if yo're hankerin' after a leetle romancin'.'

'Yu hanker after any more romancin' an' I'll hang yore hide on the livery stable wall for the whole town to see!' swore Sim Cotton. 'This is our town. We got it like that.' He held out his open hand and clenched it like a fist. 'All we got to do is get them nesters riled up enough to send for the John Laws an' we'll have more trouble than the Apaches ever gave Paw in a lifetime.'

'Hell, Sim, we could take care o' any Johnny Law that showed his nose in this valley, *an'* make it look good,' protested Art.

'Shore,' said Sim Cotton, with heavy scorn. 'That's smart thinkin', ain't it? They send in a John Law an' yu want to burn him down. What happens then, Brains? What's the next thing happens? I'll tell yu: they send in another. And another, or two, or three. An' then the whole thing is shot. I ain't about to lose this valley now not when the whole thing is going to pay off, after all these years. I ain't goin' to lose it, yu hear me? Not for some wet-nosed nester's brat who ain't even got blood in her veins.' He looked threateningly at Buck Cotton. 'If yu ever set foot on Lazy H land again, without my say-so, boy, I'll *make yu regret it.*'

The spaced, evenly measured lack of violence in his words turned Buck Cotton's face pale, and he nodded.

'Yu got my word, Sim,' he managed.

'An yu got mine, little brother,' replied Sim. 'Bite on it.'

Art Cotton stood up and yawned. He wandered across to the window and looked out down the street. Mott's house stood next to the bank, at the northern end of the town's curving street. From this window, the whole street was visible.

'Town's nice'n quiet,' remarked Art. 'Yu reckon that kid's nester friends'll try to cause any trouble?'

'Not if they know what's good for 'em,' Sim Cotton said. 'Besides, Helm'll have him out o' here tonight.'

'I wish yu'd let *me* take care o' that one,' muttered Buck Cotton.

'I ain't lettin' yu, or Art get involved in any o' this,' growled Sim Cotton. 'We're playin' for bigger stakes than the satisfaction o' gettin' even with some two-bit nester. When that dam goes up at Twin Peaks, this valley is goin' to be worth more money than yu've ever dreamed was printed. This town is goin' to boom, an' we're goin' to be holdin' all the aces. We can put our own price on the land, on the buildin', on everything!' His eyes gleamed avariciously as he allowed his thoughts to formulate pictures before his eyes. 'But it ain't certain until next month. An' until next month we got to keep the lid tight on this town. Any sign o' trouble, an' Chris Helm steps in. Let him. If the John Laws come in, Helm's the one caused all the trouble. I got a paper showin' him hired out to Harry Parris as a deputy for the last two years!' He laughed evilly. 'We'll be in the clear. It'll all be ours! Every inch o' this rotten fleabag of a town'll be worth its weight in diamonds.'

For a long moment, the fever of greed burned in his close-set eyes, then slowly died away, and he turned to Buck Cotton.

'Get out o' here,' he said. There was a tone of something as close to affection as Sim Cotton could get. 'Tell Chris Helm I want to see him.'

Buck Cotton nodded, and went out, thankful to be released from his brother's baleful gaze. In a few minutes, a discreet knock at the door which led directly on to the side alley from the room announced the arrival of the tall gunfighter. He ducked under the door lintel and nodded. 'Sim, Art. Ol' Martin did a fine job o' speechifyin' at the Oasis. I got him out o' there afore his tongue got stuck in the bottle.'

Sim Cotton looked up sharply. 'Drunken ol' fool,' he snapped. 'He give yu any trouble?'

'Shucks, no,' shrugged Helm. 'I just pointed him at his bed, an' tapped him one behind the ear with this—' He touched the barrel of one of his sixguns. 'He'll wake up thinkin' he swilled too much rotgut.'

Sim Cotton nodded. He stood up and paced the width of the room three times before turning to face the gunfighter again.

'This kid,' he began. 'I want yu to take care o' things.'

37

Helm nodded, his face unperturbed.

'Yu reckon Harry's boys might botch it? They ain't yet.'

'I want to be shore on this, Helm. That boy's a firebrand. If he was to go shootin' off his mouth, it could do us a lot o' harm.'

'I reckon,' was Helm's uncritical reply. 'Leave it to me. I'll see he don't cause you no trouble, Sim.'

Cotton nodded. Helm stood to go, then hesitated. Art Cotton looked up at the tall gunfighter.

'That other feller,' Helm began. 'Green, he said his name was.'

'What about him?'

'I had the feelin' I've seen him someplace. Can't put a finger on it. But . . . aw, hell, probably just imagination.'

'No, wait,' Sim Cotton held up a hand. 'Where do yu reckon yu've run across this jasper? Is he a lawman?'

Helm shook his head. 'No, I don't reckon so. But I got the hunch I've seen him someplace. Texas, mebbe. It'll come to me.'

'It don't matter a hell of a lot,' Art Cotton laughed coldly. 'He'll be snake bait by now.' They joined in his mirthless laughter. Then Sim Cotton pulled out the elegant silver watch from his waistcoat pocket. 'One-thirty,' he announced. 'Let's go an' eat.'

Thus callously did the lord of the valley dismiss from his thoughts the murderous deeds which had sprung from his dark plotter's mind. He had just condemned Billy Hornby to death. In the fate of the other man, Green, he had no further interest. As Art Cotton had said, Green was already snake bait.

CHAPTER FIVE

'This'll do. Get down, Green.'

Dan's command, when it came, was almost a relief after the endless tension of the miles they had ridden from town. Green turned to see the other deputy, Norris, unstrapping from behind his saddle a small folding shovel, such as the United States Cavalry carried on field expeditions.

'Get down, I said!' The repeated command was emphasised by a gesture with the shotgun. Green shrugged, and lifted his leg over the saddle horn, sliding down to the ground effortlessly despite his bound hands. As he did so, Dan covered him without dismounting, while Norris dismounted, dropped the shovel on the ground, and walking in a wide, half-circle, never coming between the two men, sidled up behind Green.

'Stick yore arms out behind yu,' he ordered, and when Green complied, slashed the puncher's bonds apart with two deft strokes of the knife. Green stood kneading the cramped muscles of his arms as Norris unhurriedly stepped backwards, away from him, as unhurriedly unhitched the shotgun from where it hung on the saddle horn by a leather loop, and covered Green as Dan dismounted.

Dan motioned towards the shovel. 'Start diggin',' he told Green

'My arms is mighty cramped, boys,' Green remonstrated. 'Give me a minnit to get 'em workin' again.'

'Start diggin',' snapped Norris. 'That oughta do it.' He smiled evilly at his companion, who grinned back.

Green stretched his arms to their fullest extent. Then he placed his hands on his hips and faced his captors.

'Yu boys aimin' to kill me in cold blood?'

'Dig!' Again the gesture with the shotgun.

'I'd as lief not bother,' snapped Green. 'If yo're aimin' to perforate me, I'm shore as hell not goin' to dig my own grave.'

The man called Dan looked at his fellow-deputy and put on a resigned expression.

'Why do we allus get the argumentary ones?' he asked.

'Beats me,' admitted Norris.

'Yu reckon we can talk him out o' his bad mood?'

Norris grinned evilly. 'We could shore try. What yu wanna do? Shall I hold him, or will yu?'

Dan grinned. His thick, stubbled chin dropped, revealing broken teeth, and Green realised that the man was one of those barroom toughs who relished nothing more than beating a defenceless man, or a weaker one, into a bloody, whimpering pulp.

'Just keep that cannon pointed at him, an' move to the side a bit,' grinned Dan. 'I'll see if I can't talk him out o' this bad mood he's in. Make him a mite more co-operative.'

'Yeah, yu do that. On'y leave some for me, Dan. Don't go breakin' his leg or nothin'.'

'Shore, Jerry, shore,' mumbled the deputy. He laid down his shotgun, while Green's mind raced. The reference that Norris had just made: could it be that this was the man who had crippled the doctor, the one that Billy had told him about? His eyes narrowed; he had no time to think any more about it, for Dan was shambling forward.

'C'mon, cowboy,' he mouthed. 'Give me an argyment.'

'Shore,' Green replied. 'Let me just get my bearin's.' Gauging his distance carefully, the puncher took three rapid steps, bringing himself almost directly between Dan and Norris. With a curse, Norris dropped his indolent pose and skipped hastily to one side, trying to get a clear aim at Green, and yelling 'Dan! Hit the floor, Dan!' But even as the words left his lips, Green was moving forward, fast and hard and low, flinging himself directly into the arms of the lumbering Dan, who reacted exactly as Green had figured he would, by wrapping his huge arms about the body of the puncher and exerting a bone-cracking bear hug, designed to snap his enemy's spine. An evil growl escaped his corded throat, and he was oblivious to his companions' yells.

'Drop him, Danny,' yelled Norris. 'Let him go, yu dumb ape! Let me get a shot at him.'

He danced to one side, the twin hammers of the shotgun fully cocked, as deadly as a barracuda. His shouts penetrated his sidekick's murder-addled brain, and Dan shook his head angrily realising the trick that the puncher, now writhing in his punishing grip, had played on him. He loosened his grasp slightly, confused by Norris's shouts, unsure of whether he had been tricked or not, and in that moment of loosening pressure, Green acted.

With every ounce of strength he could muster, he heaved upwards with his right hand cupped, the heel of his palm catching the deputy flush beneath his bearded jaw, racking his head back with a huge jolt, stunning even that great bear of a man and sending him flailing backwards, while Green fell away and sideways out of his grip, flicking Dan's revolver out of the holster at his side, firing almost beneath Dan's arm at the menacing figure of Jerry Norris. His shot took the deputy between the eyes, blasting the man backwards dead on his feet as Green hit the ground. Norris's fingers tightened in muscular spasm on the twin triggers of the shotgun as he fell backwards, and the huge *boomf!* of the twin cartridges was shocking in the silence of the badlands.

The shot from both barrels took Dan off his feet like a puppet thrown from a train, and he went over sidewards in a tattered heap, smashing into a pile of fumbled rocks and going over them in a welter of arms and legs.

Green picked himself warily up, the .45 cocked and ready in his hand. A quick glance at Norris showed that the man was dead, and Green moved carefully over to where Dan had tumbled across the rocks. The man lay in a shattered heap where he had fallen. Green shook his head.

'Never thought yu'd fall for that one, boys,' he managed. He picked up Norris's shotgun and reloaded it, gathered up the other shotgun, stripped the gunbelt from the fallen

Norris, and strapped it on his own waist. The second .45 he stuck into his waistband.

'Ain't quite like havin' my own guns,' he said to nobody in particular. 'But it shore is an improvement over an hour ago.' He walked over to where the horses stood, eyes still rolling in fear from the explosions, blessing the training which had kept them 'ground-hitched' despite their terror, by the trailing reins. In another moment he was mounted. His gaze fell upon the shovel, lying upon the ground, and then rose to the black, wheeling dots already circling in the sky. The buzzards always knew.

He hesitated for a long moment. Then he shook his head.

'Yu boys knew what yu was gettin' into,' he said aloud. 'I shore hate to do it, but . . .'

With a shrug he caught up the reins of his horse and thundered off without a backward glance, heading north. Behind him the buzzards floated down and settled in a live oak tree to wait in their eternal patience for the silence to return.

CHAPTER SIX

The afternoon sun beat down on Cottontown. Along the curve of the street the sidewalks were deserted. A small grey dog lay panting in the shade thrown by the awning of the livery stable, but otherwise no sound nor movement disturbed the stillness. In appearance, Cottontown was typical of a hundred other Western settlements. Along its single street straggled a variety of squat unlovely buildings, some of them slightly more imposing than others. They faced each other across a wide strip of wheel-rutted, hoof-pocked dust, the absence of paint remedied by the grey-white alkali dust which covered everything, and the rubble of refuse which hemmed in each habitation forming a sordid substitute for vegetation.

Looking north along Cottontown's street, the largest building on the left was the wide, low-built jail, with the sheriff's house just to the north of it, and beyond that the frame shack which housed Judge Kilpatrick. Opposite the jail was the livery stable, while the Oasis, with its peeling false front and grimy windows, directly faced the sheriff's house, a fact which had not escaped the notice of some of Cottontown's more daring wits. The banker, Mott, lived on the northern end of the town, between the bank, which stood next to the saloon, and opposite the general store. His bank, in fact, was the most substantial building in the town. Apart from these larger buildings, only a straggle of houses, 'dobes, even one or two dugouts, housed the remainder of Cottontown's population, while the spaces between were littered with tin cans, bottles, even the odd tumbleweed which had lodged against a building.

Green surveyed the scene from a vantage point in cool

shadow beneath the trestles of the wooden bridge spanning the Bonito. 'An' only man is vile,' he quoted. 'Shore ain't no oil paintin'.' His horse nickered and he clamped a firm hand across its nostrils. 'Easy, Thunder.' he scolded. 'They'll know soon enough that we're here. Now where did the kid say this doctor lived?' Scanning the scene before him, his keen eyes presently espied a small frame house on the southern side of the town. Its general air of neatness, and the white picket fence set it apart from most of the other dwellings. A horse stood hipshot at the hitching rail, beneath the shadow of a young cottonwood planted in the front garden of the house.

'That'll be her,' Green told himself.

Tying Thunder firmly to one of the stanchions of the bridge, he waded up the bank of the river, and moved down a gully which looked as if it might have been a small tributary of the Bonito. It led northward towards the doctor's house, and within a few minutes, Green found himself within four or five yards from it. A quick sprint across the open ground brought him noiselessly to the rear door. He knocked quietly, breathing a prayer that Hight would be alone. His hand hovered close to the gun at his side.

After a moment he heard a movement within, and the door opened. Green found himself face to face with a youngish man of medium height, about thirty years of age. The dark hair was already touched with grey, and the eyes behind the steel-rimmed spectacles were older and wiser than their owner's age might have indicated.

'Yes?' There was no more than mild curiosity in the doctor's voice.

'Can I come in?'

'What do you want?'

'Doc, my name's Green. Does that mean anything to yu?'

Hight's face was puzzled for a moment, then light suddenly came into his eyes and he threw the door open wide. 'The one who helped Billy! My God, you'd better come in – and quick,' he gasped. He scanned the area behind the house as he closed the door, and then moved to a window to survey the deserted street.

'Did anyone see you coming here?' he asked, then without waiting for an answer, 'Are you out of your mind, coming back? What are you doing here?'

'No to the first, no to the second,' was the smiling reply. 'As to the third, I've come to get the boy.'

'My God, Green, are you mad? The town is full of Cotton's men. How do you know I don't belong to them as well?'

'I'm bettin' my life on it,' was the quiet answer, and Hight was silent for a moment.

'The boy told you about me, did he?' At Green's nod, Hight went on, 'It's true. I've got my reasons for hating their guts, Mister Green, but—'

'My friends call me Jim, Doc.'

'Allright, Gr– Jim.' He smiled briefly, then put another question.

'How did you get away from those two thugs of deputies?'

'They was unavoidably detained,' was the terse reply. Hight's face took on a new, almost hopeful look.

'That . . . Dan Rodgers. Is he . . . ?'

'Dead, Doc. He's beaten up his last medico.'

Hight started visibly at these words. 'How did you know that?' he asked nervously. 'I've never told a soul about . . .'

'Dan mentioned it . . . afore he was took bad,' Green told him, then changed the subject. 'Is Billy still in the jail?'

'Yes, as far as I know.'

'How many men guardin' him?'

Hight shook his head. 'I've got no idea, Jim.'

'Don't want to go in blind,' muttered Green. 'Might be worse'n useless.' He sat silently for a moment, pondering his next move, while Hight looked at him as if he had announced his decision to fly to Santa Fe.

'Jim – you're not serious! You don't think one man alone could go into that jail and get out of Cottontown alive, do you?'

Green didn't answer, but shrugged. 'I can't leave the kid in there,' was his only comment.

'It's madness!' snapped Hight. 'You can't do it!'

'Who'd yu reckon can, then?' asked the puncher flatly, and

Hight fell silent. 'I'm sorry, Doc,' apologised Green. 'That wasn't intended personal.'

'Hell, I know that, Jim,' Hight told him. 'But one man, even if he was backed up by six others, wouldn't have much chance against Cotton's gunfighters.'

'He hire guns, then?' Green was interested in the news.

'Yes,' answered the doctor. 'Three or four of his riders are paid killers, like the two who – what happened out there, Jim?'

'They aimed to cut me down an' bury me, I changed their plans a mite,' was all Green would tell him. 'That tall jasper I seen at the trial. What's his name again?'

'Helm, you mean? Big man, wearing two guns?'

Green nodded. 'That's the one.'

'Name's Chris Helm. He's foreman of the Cottonwood ranch.'

'He's wanted in El Paso for murder,' Green informed the doctor.

'I'm not surprised,' replied Hight flatly.

Green took another tack. 'Billy told me somethin' about the way things are here. How long has this town been under Cotton's heel?'

'It must be ten years altogether, if you count Zeke Cotton's days as well. They own everything. Nobody can come into this valley to trade. Nobody can take anything out to sell – it all has to go through the Cottons or one of their tools. The bank, the saloon, the general store – they're all owned by the Cottons. They rent the saloon to Blass. He has to pay them a percentage of what he takes over the counter. It's their money in the bank, and they set the interest on loans.'

'An' if anyone kicks, the muscle moves in, is that it?'

'That's it. I've had experience of it – in fact, you might say I was a walking example to the rest of the town. If you call the way I get around walking.' His voice was harsh and bitter, and the memory of old pain was in the doctor's eyes.

'There are settlers to the south who have been hoping for years to come and farm in this valley. The one or two who've ventured north of the Bonito have been bullied and harassed to such an extent that they've pulled out. There used to be a

46

sign at the fork of the road, about ten miles south of town: "This is Zeke Cotton's road – take the other one." They aren't quite that obvious now, but the result's the same. Newcomers aren't encouraged to stay.'

'I know that,' murmured Green, a frosty smile playing around his lips.

'Why are you involving yourself in all this?' asked Hight suddenly. 'What does it matter to you what happens to Billy Hornby, or me, or Cottontown?'

'It's a long story, Doc. I doubt we've got time for it.'

Hight sat himself down in a chair facing Green. His face was earnest and something deeper than curiosity was in his eyes.

'Make it short, then,' he bid the puncher. 'Tell me what your interest is, and maybe I'll help you. If they're the right reasons, that is.'

'Help me? How can yu help me?' Green looked puzzled.

Hight leaned forward eagerly.

'I'll go over to the jail on some excuse, and find out how many men are in there.'

Green looked at him in amazement, then shook his head, smiling. 'An' I though this town was spineless,' he murmured. 'Yu'd do it?'

'If you tell me what I want to know.'

Green hesitated for a moment, then came to a decision.

'I'm lookin' for two men. Mebbe yu've heard o' them. Their names are Webb an' Peterson.'

Hight pondered for a moment. 'Can't say the names are familiar, but names don't mean much in these parts. What do you want them for?'

'I want to settle a debt.'

Somehow, the way in which these words were spoken put a chill in the medical man's veins. Green's eyes were cold and ruthless, and Hight did not envy the two men, whoever they were.

'Who are you, Green?' he asked bluntly.

'My name's shore 'nough Jim Green,' the puncher told him. 'But in Texas, they've given me another: there they call me "Sudden".'

Sudden! Remote though this corner of the West was, it was not so cut off from the world outside that Hight had not heard of the outlaw and gunfighter who bore the name of Sudden. So this quiet-spoken man with the level gaze, watching him now unperturbed, was the fantastic wizard whose genius with the sixgun had already earned him a place among the famous – or the infamous – of the frontier! Sudden the man who had cleaned out Lawless, the man who . . .

Green had been watching his host carefully and saw the dawning hesitation in the doctor's eyes.

'Yo're wonderin' if mebbe I ain't tarred with the same brush as them jaspers Cotton hires, ain't yu?' he said harshly. 'Yu reckon anyone with a reputation like Sudden's couldn't possibly be anythin' but what they say about him. Well, yo're goin' to hear the whole story, Doc. After that, I'm in yore han's.' Without ado, Green proceeded to recount the circumstances which had led to his infamous notoriety. The medico listened in amazement to the story of a promise made to a man on his death bed, of the blind search for two murderers that the promise bound him to, and the false accusation of murder that had sent a boy alone into the wild frontier country with a price on his head, a target for every bounty hunter and reputation-builder who crossed his track.

'Most o' what yu'll have heard about me is lies,' Sudden told the doctor. 'But some of it ain't. Yu'll jest have to make yore own mind up which is which.'

Hight did not hesitate. He thrust out his hand and grasped the other's. 'Jim, if you're Sudden, then I'm guessing most of what's said about you is lies. And—' he grinned, 'since half the world are liars, anyway, it isn't really surprising.' He limped into his study and returned with a stout walking stick. 'I think I'll just go over and see that the boy is in good hands. Tell him his sister is doing fine.' He turned at the door to face Sudden. 'Stay here. Don't show yourself. I'll be back as soon as I can.'

Sudden nodded, saying nothing, and Hight limped out into the street. So that was Sudden! The quiet, drawling voice and the casual air hardly jibed with the lurid tales he had heard about the famous outlaw. He tried to recall some of them in detail, but found he could not. Something about the Hell City business down in Arizona. But on which side: right or wrong? Good or evil? Hight squared his shoulders.

'I know where my bet's going,' he announced to nobody in particular. The grey dog in the shadow of the livery stable looked up at the sound of Hight's voice, and watched disinterestedly as the doctor limped across the street and knocked on the door of the jailhouse.

Hight was gone about fifteen minutes. Watching through the window of the medico's house, Green saw him emerge from the jail and limp across the street. Hight's progress was maddeningly casual and Green, on tenterhooks, swore and then laughed at himself.

'Gettin' all steamed up ain't goin' to help,' he muttered, and moved to meet Hight as he came in. There was a smile on the doctor's face, for his tiding were good.

'The boy's in his cell, Jim,' he announced. 'It looks as if there's only one guard.'

'Which one? Helm?'

'No, one of the others,' Hight replied. 'I think he's called Jackson. The sheriff must be having his usual siesta.'

'Let's hope we don't disturb him, then,' smiled Sudden. They shook hands warmly again. 'Thanks, Doc,' the puncher said. 'I'm hopin' there won't be no gunplay, but if yu hear shootin' keep yore head down. Act surprised if anyone asks yu about me. Yu ain't never seen me afore: sabe?'

Hight nodded. 'How about a horse for the boy?'

Green's smile was impish. 'I was plannin' on stealin' yores, Doc,' he said mischievously. 'I figgered yu'd trade for one o' Billy's. I'm shore his sister'd take yore word on it.'

He feigned not to notice the colour which rose in Hight's cheeks, but told himself that Billy's observations about the medico's feelings towards Jenny Hornby were accurate enough.

'Just as well,' he thought. 'She'll have someone to look after her if Billy has to lie low an' can't take care o' things.'

'Take the horse and welcome,' Hight was saying. 'And – good luck, Jim.'

Sudden nodded. 'I'll be needin' some,' he remarked. Without further talk he edged out of the back door of the house and moved cautiously around the side of the house into the deep shadow which lay between it and the livery stable next door. He sidled up to the corner of the stable and peered around it, keen eyes taking every inch of the curving street and its buildings. No movement caught his attention: even the grey dog had gone. The street yawned wide and empty before him.

'Hell, the longer I look at her, the wider she'll seem,' he muttered. Tipping his Stetson forward over his eyes, and sticking his hands casually into his hip pockets, Sudden sauntered into the street. Every nerve was tense, keyed for instant action at the first sight of danger, but outwardly his air was one of complete unconcern. He looked like a man who had every right to be where he was, doing what he was doing. 'They'd spot a fella runnin' in a couple o' seconds,' was his reasoning. 'But someone walkin' natural attracts no attention – I hope!' A few more moments and he was across. With something like a sigh of relief he stepped up on to the porch of the jailhouse and knocked on the door.

A chair shifted inside the jail, and footsteps approached the door, stopping behind it.

'Who's there?' called a man's voice.

'Helm, Jackson,' Sudden said gruffly. 'Open up!'

He heard the bolts being withdrawn behind the door, which opened about three inches to reveal a whiskery face peering around the edge. The bulging eyes crossed along the barrel of Green's .45, cocked and deadly which he had whipped upwards to almost touch the man's nose.

'One sound an' yo're the *late* Mr Jackson,' Sudden grated. 'Open up an' back in!'

Jackson complied, his eyes still bugging at the appearance of this man he thought long since murdered.

'Yo're thinkin' I'm mebbe a ghost?' jibed Sudden. Indeed, Jackson's hands were trembling as if Green were a real apparition.

'Turn around!' snapped Sudden, and the man complied

hastily. A merciless blow with the barrel of the .45 dropped Jackson like a sack of flour on the floor. Rummaging around Sudden found some rawhide thongs in a drawer of the sheriff's desk, and efficiently bound Jackson's hands and feet. A tight gag completed the work, leaving Sudden free to spend another two or three minutes finding his own guns and gunbelt. Strapping them on, he moved cat-footed into the corridor which led to the cells. Memory guided him to the door, and he slammed the bolts back, swinging the door wide to reveal Billy Hornby sitting with his head in his hands, gazing morosely at the floor.

'Yu'll never win my heart with a face like that,' Sudden said, and almost burst out laughing at Billy's exaggerated reaction to seeing him in the doorway.

'Jim!' gasped the boy. 'How in the name o'—'

'All done by mirrors,' Green told him. 'Less questions an' more action. On yore feet – here catch!' he tossed the boy his spare gunbelts and guns, the ones he had stripped from the scar-faced Norris. 'Time to get out o' here, afore Sleepin' Beauty wakes up,' he told Billy.

'Jim, never thought I'd see yu again,' Billy said, as he strapped on the gunbelt. 'How in tarnation did yu get loose?'

He slapped the holsters into a comfortable position and looked up as Green said 'Later. First of all we got to get clear o' here. Listen to me: across the street a hoss is tethered. It's Doc Hight's. Walk across there. Don't run, don't even move fast. Act as natural as yu can. I'm goin' around the back to get my hoss down at the bridge. When yu get on the hoss outside the Doc's walk him down to the bridge. By that time I'll be mounted up. As soon as yu see me, turn him loose an' head after me. Yu got it straight?'

He looked keenly at the boy, who seemed preoccupied with other thoughts.

Billy looked up blankly. 'Oh: shore, Jim. Don't worry none.'

'Yu allright, Billy?' the puncher asked.

Billy looked surprised. He slapped the guns at his side. 'Shore, Jim. I'm fine, now. Go on, we better git movin'.'

Frowning slightly, Sudden opened the rear door of the jailhouse and after checking that the coast was clear, edged along the back of the building and across the open land towards the declivity which bordered the river. He slid down it, watching from the corner of his eye for Billy to appear by the horse outside the doctor's house. The boy was not yet in sight, perhaps blocked from Sudden's view by the bulk of the jail. He sloshed through the shallows of the river to where Thunder stood patiently awaiting his master. He was just about to untie the reins when he heard Billy Hornby's clear young voice yelling:

'Buck Cotton! Come out here!'

The boy had gone back to the saloon.

CHAPTER SEVEN

Buck Cotton was not in the Oasis. He had left town for the ranch with his two brothers perhaps half an hour before Sudden had released Billy Hornby from the jail, immediately after Sim Cotton had given some special instructions to the Sheriff.

The conference had taken place in Mott's house, the banker sitting quietly in a corner of his own parlour, his eyes huge as he listened to what Sim Cotton was saying. Harry Parris stood, threading the brim of his hat through nervous fingers, around and around, licking his lips occasionally but otherwise silent.

'I want that kid out o' my hair,' rumbled Sim Cotton. 'Yu savvy, Harry? I want him gone – no more problems, no more wild talk, no gossip, just gone. I'm leavin' Helm to help yu.'

Parris's eyes met Helm's briefly. He wanted to protest, but something in the man's flat gaze stopped him.

'Yu don't need to do that, Sim,' he said, a faint air of complaint in his voice. 'My boys can take care o' things.'

'Mebbe they'll be tired after their long ride,' Helm put in quietly. 'It's hard work. Yore boys didn't ought to have to do all the hard work, Harry.'

'They ain't—'

'Yore boys, that's right,' snapped Sim Cotton. 'So what I say goes, right? An' what I say is, I want this job done properly. Which means I want Helm to handle it.'

'I wish yu'd let me take care o' that son-of-a-itch,' Buck Cotton interposed. 'I shore owe him somethin'.'

'Yu?' Sim Cotton laughed out loud. 'From what I hear yu

was wettin' yore pants when he came after yu with a gun in the Oasis. Hell, boy, I wouldn't put yu in charge o' drowning three kittens in a gunnysack!'

Buck Cotton's face set angrily, and he bit his lips. He knew better than to retort, however. Being Sim Cotton's brother would not exclude him from Sim's violent methods of dealing with anyone who opposed his dictator's will.

'Well, whatever yu say, Sim,' Parris said, eventually. 'Although I can't see. . . .'

'Yu don't have to see,' was the brutal rejoinder. 'Yu just do what I tell yu, yu broken-down imitation.'

Parris bridled at this tongue lashing. 'Now see here, Sim, there ain't no call to take that kind o' line with me. I—' he stopped in mid-sentence. Sim Cotton was regarding him with baleful eyes, and Art was leaning forward in his chair with a peculiar light dancing in his eyes.

'Yu want me to talk to Harry some, Sim?' asked Art. Parris went cold at these words. Art Cotton was one of the dirtiest, roughest fist-fighters he had ever seen in action; Paris was sure the cold light in his eyes came from a pathological hatred of his fellow man. Art Cotton was never happier than when he was using his hands. Parris had seen him once beat up a man they had caught with two stolen Cottonwood steers in his possession. Art had systematically, scientifically beaten the man into a raw and bleeding pulp, whimpering for mercy, helpless, blinded in his own blood. And the man had been hard, tough – and nobody had held him. He looked beseechingly at Sim Cotton.

'No need for that, Art,' rumbled the rancher, and a great sigh of relief escaped involuntarily from Parris's fat lips. 'Harry's scared enough just thinkin' about it.' The rancher laughed aloud, an ugly sound.

'All right, there's nothin' else for us to do here. I'm headin' back for the ranch. Yu, Buck, leave yore horse here. Helm'll need a better nag than he's got, to get back to the ranch by tomorrow. I want yu to get back as fast as yu can, Helm. Art, yu stay here – make shore everything's taken care of, an' properly. Bucky, let's go.'

They got their horses and rode out of town, leaving one of the Cottonwood riders with Helm and Art Cotton. After their departure, the three Cottonwood men went down the street to the saloon. They were playing a desultory game of monte over a drink when Billy Hornby's words sliced the silence of the afternoon.

As the boy's challenge rang in the still room, the rider, whose name was Ricky, was lolling backwards on his upright chair. He went over backwards in a flailing, startled welter of arms and legs. Art Cotton swore at him and struggled to disentangle himself from the man's grasp, for Ricky had clutched at him as he fell, almost dragging Art to the floor with him. Blass, who had been polishing glasses behind his bar, froze in mid-polish, but did not fail to notice that Helm had risen to his feet in one smooth movement, the right hand gun snaked from the tooled holster without apparent thought.

'Well, well,' said Helm in amazement, as Cotton and Ricky scrambled to their feet. 'It sounds as if our li'l rabbit done broke out o' his hutch.' He turned to the bartender. 'Don't yu make the mistake o' openin' yore squawkbox,' he warned Blass. 'Or yu'll be out of a job an' the undertaker'll be in one.'

Outside the saloon, Billy repeated his challenge, misled by the presence of Buck Cotton's horse at the hitching rail.

Helm turned to his companions. 'Art, yu an' Ricky sidle out the back door. Git aroun' behind him. I reckon we'll have ourselves a passel o' fun trimmin' this young rooster's comb!'

He made an impatient gesture with his hand, and the two men nodded and sidled out of the saloon through the back entrance while Helm moved swiftly, silently, tall and catlike, towards the batwing doors. The bartender glanced helplessly towards the window.

'Yu on'y get one warnin', boy,' Helm said, sibilantly, and shook a warning finger. His voice was almost playful, but Blass was not fooled. He knew that any attempt to warn Billy Hornby would result in his own death. The bartender was brave enough, but he was not a fool. He stayed rooted to the spot.

'Whatever yu say, Helm,' he managed, hoarsely.

Helm nodded, and then ignoring the bartender, pushed

out through the batwings on to the sidewalk, his thumbs hooked in his fancy belt.

'Bucky ain't here, sonny,' he told Billy softly. 'But I am.'

He stepped down off the sidewalk into the dusty street, took three paces forward, and stopped. His demeanour was casual, unperturbed. He had the situation under control. Billy glanced nervously up and down the empty street. He had not been prepared for the appearance of the gunfighter. He took an uncertain step.

'Yu goin' someplace?' Helm's question was delivered in an unemphatic tone. Only the man's eyes belied the offhand words. They were cold and deadly.

Billy frowned, nonplussed. He knew he could handle a gun reasonably well enough to possibly outdraw Buck Cotton – but a professional gunman was another matter. Against this man he would have no chance. A movement to one side caught his attention, and dismay spread across his face as Art Cotton and the man called Ricky stepped out from the shadowed alley between the saloon and the livery stable. They made no overt move, but walked coolly out into the street, parting slightly to spread around the boy, making him shift his position to keep them in sight. Helm grinned like a hunting coyote.

'Yu didn't even have brains enough to run,' he grated. 'Who turned yu loose?'

Billy shook his head. Maybe Green had got clear.

'Yu better tell us, boy,' rasped Art Cotton. 'It has to be some-one in this town. Whoever it was, we'll be wantin' to talk to him.'

'I . . . I got loose on my own,' protested Billy. 'Nobody helped me.'

Cotton nodded, his face disbelieving. 'Ricky, go take a look in the jail.' The Cottonwood rider nodded, and hastened off across the street towards the jail.

Art Cotton took several paces forward, until he was almost near enough to Billy to reach out and touch him.

'That's far enough!' snapped the boy. 'Keep back!'

'O-ho,' smiled Helm, mirthlessly. 'Cat's got teeth.'

'Yu aimin' to draw on me, sonny?' asked Art Cotton, his

56

voice flat. 'Even if yu could outdraw me – which I misdoubt – yu reckon yu can beat Helm?'

Billy shook his head.

'I don't reckon,' he said. 'But I'll take yu with me if yu come one step closer!'

Cotton smiled. The expressionless eyes bored into those of the youngster. He took a step forward.

'Don't take another, Cotton!'

The voice from across the street was icy with menace, and it froze Art Cotton where he stood. Helm wheeled to face this new challenge, his hands flashing towards his guns. He too froze as he saw the rock-steady twin revolvers in Sudden's hands. He shrugged and relaxed his crouched stance. His eyes flickered over towards the jail as Sudden approached cautiously from his position at the corner of the sheriff's house. Sudden saw the look and a sardonic smile touched his grim lips.

'If yo're hopin' yore rider's goin' to bail yu out, forget it,' he told Helm. 'He had an overpowerin' urge to lie down.' He gestured with his right hand gun. 'Damn near bent the barrel.'

A curse escaped Art Cotton. 'So that's how the boy got loose,' he swore. 'An' that means Norris an' Rodgers is cashed, too, I'm takin' it.'

'Yo're takin' it correct,' Sudden told him. 'But yu don't seem to be takin' it too hard.'

'If yu got them, they musta been fools,' snarled Cotton.

'They worked for yu,' was the telling reply. 'Which don't point to them bein' over-bright. All right, enough jabber. Shuck yore guns – both o' yu. An' mind how yu do it.'

With a muttered imprecation, Art Cotton unbuckled his gunbelt and allowed it to fall to the dusty ground. Helm's hand moved too, because for a fraction of a second, Sudden's eyes had flicked across to watch Cotton step away from his guns.

In that half-second, Helm's hands flashed towards his guns and were on the butts, lifting them level, when Sudden leaped forward, the barrel of his right hand gun describing a short, vicious arc. The heavy weapon caught Helm above the right ear and dropped him to his knees, stunned. He half fell forward, one gun still in his hand, trying to bring it up to sight it at the man in front of him. Once again, the barrel of Sudden's gun flickered in the sunlight, and Helm went down like a poleaxed steer.

'Some fellers is hard to convince,' Sudden remarked casually. He cast a glance about him. 'Where's yore brothers, mister?' he asked the disarmed Art Cotton.

'They ain't here, damn yore eyes!' grated Art. 'Or yu'd be whistlin' a different tune!'

'Had it all worked out, didn't yu?' was the sardonic reply. 'Helm takes the kid for a short ride, like the one Norris an' Rodgers took me for. Then yu go back to rawhidin' this town. Somebody oughta cut yu *hombres* down to size.'

Art Cotton spat disgustedly. 'Big talk when yu got the drop, mister,' he sneered. 'Yu wouldn't talk so loud if yu wasn't hidin' behind that gun.'

His boastful words carried clearly to the knot of spectators who had appeared on the sidewalk as if they had in some mysterious way sensed the drama which was taking place in the dusty street. A thought struck Sudden.

'Billy,' he snapped. 'Hop over to the sheriff's house an' invite him to join us. If he gives yu an argument, persuade him to come anyhow.' A grin appeared on Billy's face, and he wheeled to do Sudden's bidding. In a few moments he was back, herding the discomfited Parris in front of him. Parris's face was bloated, his hair awry.

'He was takin' a nap,' explained Billy. 'Snorin' like a sheep.'

Cotton looked at the sheriff disgustedly. 'Sleepin' was yu?' he raged. 'This jasper's treein' yore town, an' yu lie there snorin' yore thick head off.'

'Art, I . . . I didn't expect . . .' mumbled Parris.

'Yu stupid clod!' hurled Cotton. 'Yu wouldn't expect it to snow in the winter!' He turned to face Sudden again. 'As for yu, mister, yu better get on yore hoss an' head for the hills. Yu beat the game once, but yu ain't likely to get away with it a second time.'

Sudden smiled at him, although the smile did not each his eyes.

'Yo're forgettin' I'm the one with the gun,' he pointed out.

'I ain't forgettin' anything,' snapped Art Cotton. 'Yu got a tiger by the tail. So you got the drop on me. So, big deal. Now what yu aimin' to do – shoot me down in the street?'

'Don't tempt me,' was the rejoinder, and the icy words brought a startled look to Art Cotton's face. He countered it with bluff.

'Mister, this is our town. Yu expect help from these sheep?' He gestured contemptuously towards the knot of watchers. 'They wouldn't lift a finger to help yu.'

'I ain't feelin' the need o' help,' Sudden pointed out. 'How about yu?'

Cotton shrugged. 'If yu was half a man, an' wasn't hidin' behind yore gun, mebbe we could settle this different.' A malignant gleam of cunning entered his eyes, which turned to triumph as Sudden nodded.

'Yu may be right at that,' said the puncher. 'I'm guessin' that Cottonwood needs to see one o' the Cottons crawl. Mebbe this is as good a time as any for them to see it.'

So saying, he holstered his guns and then unbuckled the twin belts and tossed them to one side. Billy voiced a protest as he did so.

'Jim, don't! It's just what he wants you to do.'

'Shet yore face, sonny!' growled Cotton. 'I'll come to yu when I've taken care o' yore big-talkin' friend here.'

'First catch yore hare,' taunted Sudden, and without warning stepped in and felled Art Cotton with a short, right-armed uppercut which sent the Cottonwood man reeling backwards into the dirt, spitting blood from his broken lips. With a curse that was almost a scream, Cotton lurched to his feet, and rushed at the slim man who stood poised before him. Sudden let him come, almost until Cotton's clutching hands had taken hold of him. Then he stepped swiftly aside and again felled his opponent with a clubbed fist. Cotton ploughed face down into the dirt once more. He lay there for a moment, shaking his head, spitting dirt from his mouth.

'By Gawd!' yelled one bystander, unable to contain himself and disregarding his ingrained fear of the Cottons. 'He's beat already!' Cotton scrambled to his feet, throwing a wicked look at the knot of watchers.

'I'll find the man who said that!' he snarled. 'After I've showed yu where this jasper steps off when he ain't got a gun.'

'Yu talk a good fight, Cotton,' jibed Sudden. 'Yu ain't caught yore hare yet.'

Cotton glowered at his opponent for a second. Dropping his head, he made a sudden plunge at Sudden, but once again the puncher was ready. He slipped easily aside and drove a fist into the thick neck, then stood waiting, a small smile of derision on his face. Cotton shook his head and charged again. Again Sudden stopped him, without so much as suffering a glancing blow. Again Cotton rushed in, again the other planted a punishing blow and slipped aside. Cotton growled; these tactics did not suit his style of fighting at all. The watchers, too, became impatient.

'Stand up an' fight,' someone called. 'This ain't no dancin' contest.'

Billy Hornby cocked his gun, and the silence became intense as the two men shuffled for position.

'Next jasper opens his mouth better have somethin' to say!' warned the boy. Nobody met his eye; the watchers were engrossed in the next stage of the fight, for the puncher, disregarding his own intuitive knowledge that Cotton preferred to fight close, had stepped forward after his man, driving Cotton backwards, trading blow for wicked blow, taking whatever Cotton gave without once ceasing to land punishment upon the retreating cowman.

The fight became one of blind fury. Cotton now slithered to one knee, and Sudden stepped back for a moment, to reveal the marks that Cotton had put on him. A jagged cut from which dark blood oozed marked the cowboy's brow, and there was a purple lump at the ridge of his jaw. Cotton was in worse shape, if anything. One eye was swollen, almost completely shut, and a huge welt the size of half an egg bulged his eyebrow forward. His lips were torn and bloody, and his face was scratched and puffed. Sweat and dirt had matted his hair, and white streaks lined his face where perspiration had channelled downwards through the dust from the street which darkened his visage. He knelt, panting, for a moment, one hand flat on the ground for support. Then, in a blur of movement, he came upwards at Sudden, his right hand shooting forward and hurling the dust he had grasped in it straight into the puncher's eyes.

Blinded, Sudden threw up his hands desperately as the Cottonwood man rushed in, landing murderous, crashing blows to the puncher's head. Sudden reeled backwards, his legs going from under him, pawing at his streaming eyes, able only to see a blur of movement as he fell, twisting to avoid that stomping heel which jarred into the dust where he had been a second before. Ere he could regain his feet, however, Cotton caught him in a grip like that of a grizzly bear. Vainly he struggled to free his trapped arms from the terrible pressure which was crushing his rib cage. Cotton, his expressionless eyes now alight with murderous, triumphant rage, teeth bared like those of a wolf, and the fetid breath exploding from his tattered lips, slowly tightened his hold. 'Yu got him, Art!' screeched a voice. 'Break him in two!' In that moment, Sudden's vision cleared, and he caught a momentary glimpse of the gloating face of the sheriff.

Suddenly he let his whole body go limp. The abrupt downward drag took Cotton off guard, and he stumbled. As they fell, Sudden heaved Cotton up and to the side so that as they hit the ground they were separated, enabling the puncher to roll free. He got to one knee as Cotton leapt up and turned, pivoting on one foot and driving a wicked kick straight at Sudden's head. Had it landed, the fight would have been over then and there, but Sudden saw it coming, and ducking under it, grasped Art Cotton's leg and heaved on it. Cotton went somersaulting over backwards, landing with a dull thump on his back and shoulders, raising a small cloud of dust. Sudden got up, weak still and dizzy, to stand waiting.

'Jim!' called Billy eagerly. 'Finish him off!'

Sudden shook his head and managed a lopsided grin.

'I don't fight that way,' he gasped, and the boy cursed his friend's idea of fair play, knowing that if the circumstances had been reversed, Cotton would have tromped him like a sidewinder.

Art Cotton soon recovered. The shock of the fall, which had stunned him momentarily was dissipated, and with a spat curse he clambered to his feet.

'That was a mistake, cowboy!' he jeered. Sinking his head, he charged in again, right fist hurtling forward to deliver a blow which would have dropped an ox. It never landed. Sudden swayed to let the murderous punch slide underneath his arm, and clasping both hands together in a doubled fist, chopped downwards at Cottons' exposed neck. Cotton dropped to his knees, his eyes glazed. Sudden stooped downward, grabbed the man's shirt in his hand and hauled Cotton to his feet. The man stood tottering as Sudden chopped him with a right, then a left, then another right; short, cutting, punishing punches which never travelled more than six or seven inches but which had every ounce of his strength behind them. Cotton still stood, tottering, swaying like a tree in a high wind, blood streaming down his smashed face, both his eyes closed, his hands groping feebly for his enemy, trying to stop this blasting hurt. But now Sudden was merciless. Again he chopped Cotton to his knees. Again he hauled him up. A cold empty light was in his eyes. He once more delivered the vicious uppercuts, and Art Cotton fell again to the ground, this time sprawling on his side, head cradled in his arms.

'Stop ... please. ...' His voice was piteous. 'Don't any more.'

'Get up!' snapped Sudden. 'Yu ain't through yet.'

'No – no, no more, no more!' The words were almost a scream. Green lifted the man apparently without effort by his shirt front. Cotton cringed from the expected blow, but Sudden merely yanked him around to where the townspeople could see him.

'Here's yore unbeatable Cottons,' he told them. 'Here's the family that's been grindin' yore faces in the dirt for years.' He thrust Art Cotton forward. 'Take a good look. They ain't made o' steel. Yu can hurt them.' He gave Cotton a contemptuous shove, and the half-conscious man reeled a few paces and then stumbled over the prone form of Helm, who lay in the street where he had fallen, a thin trickle of blood drying on his face.

Cotton slid to the ground beside the gunfighter and lay there, his body heaving, racked with dry, frustrated sobs.

Sudden turned to Parris, who quailed as the puncher bent his frowning attention upon him.

'I . . . I ain't . . . it . . . I didn't . . .' he faltered.

'Get those two on their horses,' snapped Green. 'An' get them out o' here. Put the one that's sleepin' over there by the jail with them an' take them back where they belong – they're smellin' up the town. *Move*!'

Parris jumped like a startled deer, and hastened over to where Cotton lay sprawled in the dust. At Sudden's bidding, two of the bystanders helped him to get Cotton into the saddle. Helm was slung face down across his horse's back, and the still-dazed Ricky was boosted into the saddle. Someone brought Parris his placid mount. The sheriff heaved himself up and turned helplessly to the watchers.

'What am . . . what shall I tell? . . . what will Sim say when . . . ?'

'Tell him yu beat 'em up yoreself, Harry!' yelled a man in the crowd, and Sudden smiled to himself. Perhaps there was a chance yet that the townspeople would stand up against the Cottons.

'Tell Sim Cotton what happened, Parris,' he told the sheriff. 'Tell him how, an' tell him why. Most of all, tell him not to come into this town unless he's prepared to leave it in a box. Now git!'

Then he slapped the haunch of Parris's horse and that normally placid animal leaped wildly forward, almost unseating the portly sheriff. The four-horse cavalcade thundered out of town. The bartender, Blass, had watched everything that transpired through the smeared windows of the Oasis. He turned now back to his bar as the crowd in the street broke up, and the saturnine stranger who had precipitated the downfall of Art Cotton came up towards the batwing doors of the saloon.

Blass watched him as he came in, followed by the Hornby boy, who was looking at Sudden as if the cowboy had just stepped off a winged charger. Blass nodded to himself as he moved across to serve them.

'By God,' he muttered. 'I do believe there's hope for us yet!' And then he did something that nobody in Cottontown had heard for many years. Raising his voice, he called out to everyone within earshot .'Belly up, boys! The drinks are on the house!'

CHAPTER EIGHT

The Cottonwood ranch was not big, considering the range it controlled. Altogether, Sim Cotton had only fifteen men on his payroll, and this number included a cook and a horse-wrangler, neither of whom was to be considered in any way a fighting man. The cook was a grizzled oldster of perhaps sixty summers who had been badly stove-up in a stampede many years previously at Doan's Crossing on the Red River, and the wrangler was a half-Indian boy who spoke about three intelligible words in English. Sim Cotton was a calculating man. He had always believed that power was a tool, like a branding iron or a gun, to be used as necessary, in the circumstances best suited to it. Power was impersonal, and so was fear, and Sim Cotton knew how to use both. Thus had his little empire in this valley remained in his grasp long after the time when such empires had crumbled in other parts of the West. Now he stood with his back to the fireplace in the big living room of his ranch and considered the battered face of his brother Art, the fawning figure of the sheriff, and the ugly expression in the eyes of Chris Helm.

'So yu let that two-bit kid an' his sidekick run yu out o' my town?' he asked his brother mildly. There was no indication in his voice of the deep-wounded anger, the searing hurt pride inside him.

'He buffaloed me afore I seen him properly, Sim,' Helm told him. 'I was out cold the whole time him an' Art was scrappin'.' Sim Cotton's measured gaze swung towards his brother. 'An' yu . . . ?'

Art Cotton did not answer. He could not bear the truth,

65

that he had been thoroughly beaten. He could not invent a plausible enough excuse to offer his brother to explain his condition, so he simply sat, smouldering with hatred for the man who had so marked him before the entire town burning through him.

'An' our brave sheriff was sleepin'.' Sim Cotton's reptilian eyes rested now on the apprehensive Parris, who threw up his hands in front of him as though to defend himself against a blow, though Sim Cotton had not moved a finger.

'I . . . I figgered the same as yu, Sim . . . Mr Cotton . . .' he stuttered. 'That this Green feller was taken care of, an' the kid was snug in the jail . . . I just plain didn't know . . . couldn't have known . . .'

'Mebbe yo're givin' me the straightest story at that, Harry,' Sim Cotton rumbled. 'Helm here was buffaloed while he was goin' for his guns – I thought yu was supposed to be fast, Helm? An' Art got his ears beat off, an' him reckoned to be the toughest fist-fighter north o' the Rio.' He smiled, without warmth. 'I don't see how I could expect Harry to do any better than yu two misfits.' He glanced around the room.

It was a spacious room, stone floored, solid. The huge fireplace was dominated by a mounted elk's head, and scattered catamount and wolf pelts made warm splashes of fawny colour on the floor. The walls were of adobe, plastered and painted white; and the furniture, although simple, was solid and shone with the use of years. On one wall hung an oil painting of a white-bearded old man in range clothes. The artist's knowledge of the range had been limited and the background was one which would have made a real cattleman laugh, but the face of the subject had been well caught: it was a ruthless, devilish face, and the eyes were twins for those of Sim Cotton, who gazed at the picture as he spoke.

'My father built this range,' he told the men in the room: his two brothers, Helm, the sheriff, and his assembled riders. 'He made Cottonwood. He made it, an' by God, I can unmake it. If I have to, I'm hopin' I won't have to. I'm goin' to try talkin' to this man Green. I'll make no threats. But *I will have my way*!' He smashed his fist downwards upon the heavy table.

'I've waited too long to lose it now. *I will have my way!*' His youngest brother's expression caught his eye and he turned to face him.

'Buck,' he snapped. 'What's so damn funny?'

Buck Cotton stood up and stretched lazily.

'Yu,' he said, coldly. 'Yu could ride in to Cottontown an' burn it down if yu wanted to, an' nobody'd lift a finger to stop yu. Yu could ride in an' take those two out an' hang 'em in the street, an' nobody'd interfere. But no, not yu, yu let two four-flushes try to kill me, beat the hell out of Art, gunwhip yore foreman, an' run yore sheriff out o' town, and' then yu jaw about goin' in an' talkin' to them.'

Something very sudden and violent happened deep inside Sim Cotton at that moment. His affection for his kid brother was real and sincere. It had persisted out of habit long after he had learned that Buck was as unworthy of it as the meanest drunk in Cottontown. And in this moment, Sim Cotton knew that it was gone. Up to this point, he had not thought about Buck personally. The involvement of Buck in a town fracas was nothing new, but this time the events had changed the nature of things. Where normally an insult to Buck – to any of them – was an insult to all the Cottons, now he realised that this handsome youth, whose eyes were as shallow as rain, had jeopardised the future of everyone by his stupid, senseless, unnecessary attack on the girl.

Sim Cotton had worked hard to build what his father had left him into something bigger, stronger, more flexible. He had spent thousands of dollars on drinks for Congressmen and Senators in the plush clubs of Santa Fe, listening, waiting, hoping for the stray item of information which he could use, bend, turn to his own advantage. He had heard about the plans to irrigate the Bonito valley long before they had been drafted. Now, with the draft Bill to go soon before the Territorial Legislature, those years of hard work were going to pay off. But Buck – Buck had never worked in his life. His hands were as soft as those of a girl. Sim Cotton saw the danger of losing everything because his stupid kid brother couldn't be bothered to keep his hands off some nester girl. Now the work of the ranch had to be suspended; already three men were lost – maybe four if you counted Art, who looked broken – and here was Buck taunting him, daring him to ride into Cottontown and burn it to the ground, as if he were Charley Quantrill.

His calloused hand moved almost of its own accord, and his full weight was behind it. The slap caught Buck Cotton on the side of his head and lifted him physically off his feet, hurling him into the corner of the room. He slammed into the wall and slid down, huddled, tears of outrage and shock springing to his eyes, his hand scrambling for his gun which had swung around behind him with the force of his fall. In one mighty bound, Sim Cotton was towering over him, his hands clenching and unclenching, his face taut with an almost uncontrollable rage.

'Touch that gun an' I'll kill yu with my bare hands!' he hissed. Buck pulled his fingers away from the gun butt as if it had become red hot. Sim Cotton turned his back contemptuously on his brother and walked back into the centre of the silent room as though nothing had occurred. His rage was under control again, and his mind was already foraging ahead, planning, examining, discarding.

'I'm goin' in to town,' he announced. 'Yu, Helm. Ride with me. Yu too, Harry. The rest o' yu stay here. Get on with yore chores.'

One of the riders, a man called Hitchin, put in a word.

'Yu ain't aimin' to take nobody with yu, boss?'

'No,' said Cotton, his mouth closing like a trap. 'I'm goin' to call that stinkin' town's bluff. An' Mister Green's along with it!'

CHAPTER NINE

'I'm passin' a vote o' thanks to Jim Green!'

The shouted words came from the lips of Bob Davis, the storekeeper, and they drew a ragged cheer from the crowded saloon. The word of Art Cotton's beating had spread like wildfire through the town, and within half an hour of Sheriff Parris leading the battered ranch man out of town, lolling and swaying like a straw dummy on his saddle, nearly every able-bodied man in Cottontown was in the saloon, craning to get a glimpse of the cold-eyed stranger who had effected this miracle.

The object of their attention leaned against the bar, a thin smile on his lips. The bartender pounded him on the back, insisting that the puncher take another 'snort' to celebrate what he called 'the biggest day in Cottontown since the Centennial!' Even Doc Hight had hobbled in and joined the general enthusiasm. After a while, Sudden held up his hands for silence, and the forty or so men in the saloon gathered around. He hitched himself up to sit on the bar where he could see their faces, and waited until he had their complete attention.

'I'm thankin' yu gents for yore enthusiasm,' he began. 'But I'm thinkin' that lickin' one o' the Cotton brothers ain't the end o' the rope. They ain't goin' to take this lyin' down, an' that means more trouble afore we're through.'

The men nearest to Sudden shuffled their feet and looked doubtful for a moment, but someone roared out from the back: 'Let 'em come. We'll give 'em somethin' to think about!'

Another cheer greeted this hot-blooded boast, and the

69

townspeople nodded enthusiastically to each other.

'Talk's cheap!' snapped Sudden. 'I ain't sayin' yu boys don't mean what yo're sayin', but have yu given a thought to what happens if the Cottons ride in here in force? Some o' yu have got wives an' kids. If it comes to a showdown, there's goin' to be shootin', an' yu better think about it afore yu go any further!' A silence greeted these words. In truth, most of the men in the saloon had been swept along on a tide of enthusiasm composed of two parts alcohol to one part defiance. Sudden's sobering words brought them joltingly to their senses, and there was an outbreak of muttering and whispered consultation in the crowd.

'Are yu stayin' to face Cotton, Green?' asked the bearded man.

'I been in a scrap today,' Green told him, smiling, 'an' even if I won, it still feels like I lost. I'm a mite tired for runnin'.'

In the ragged cheer that followed, Billy Hornby shouted, 'I'm stickin' with Jim!'

He pushed through the crowd and placed himself by Sudden's side. In another moment the crowd parted, and Doc Hight limped forward to turn and face them. Bob Davis came forward too, and then looked expectantly at the other men.

'Ain't none o' yu comin' out here?' he faltered. The men in the front of the crowd edged backwards unable to meet his eyes. He looked at them in deep scorn.

'What kind o' town is this, anyway? Ain't yu men goin' to fight for what's yourn?'

'Hell, it's okay for yu, Bob, yu ain't got no family,' said the bearded man who had spoken earlier. 'Some of us has got little kids. We get killed, who's goin' to look after our womenfolk?'

Davis opened his mouth to say something scathing but before he could speak, Sudden intervened. 'He's right, Bob,' he told the storekeeper. 'It ain't no use expectin' to cuss him into it.' He turned to face the crowd.

'Yu boys git back to yore houses. Keep yore womenfolk an' kids off the streets until this is all over – one way or th' other.' A few men at the back of the room quickly detached themselves from the crowd and hurried out through the batwing doors. Those at the front retreated more slowly, shamefacedly, unwilling to look directly at the four men standing by the bar. Sudden turned to the bartender.

'Blass, yu better get out o' here, too,' he said.

The bartender shook his head.

'Listen, Green. Sim Cotton's bin drainin' me of every cent I make in this place these last few years. He's taken everythin' 'cept my blood. Well . . .' he reached beneath the bar and lifted out a beautifully chased shotgun which he banged on to the flat polished surface. 'I reckon it's time to find out if he wants that, too.'

He thrust out his hand and Sudden shook it warmly.

'I'm thankin' yu,' he said simply. 'I'm thankin' all o' yu.'

'Do it when it's over,' was Hight's succinct reply. 'We got to wait and see what Sim Cotton's going to do.'

Blass, who was looking idly though the window, turned suddenly towards them, his face gone pale.

'We ain't got to wait a-tall,' he whispered. 'Hyar he comes now, ridin' down the street.'

CHAPTER TEN

Sim Cotton on his palomino stallion rode easily down the street. Chris Helm rode beside him, his hands never far from the guns slung low on his hips. Parris brought up the rear, his eyes flickering nervously about, not quite meeting the half-curious, half-apprehensive stares of the townspeople who watched in silence as the Cottonwood men moved down the street. Sim Cotton could feel the eyes upon him, and it pleased him to know that his appearance with no more than a token force had created the impression he desired. He felt it was symbolic of his strength. He didn't need to ride into his own town at the head of a gang, for that would have indicated that he was unsure of himself, that this upstart kid and the slow-spoken stranger were anything other than a minor nuisance. He looked as if he had all the time, all the power he needed.

Those watching could hardly have known that time was Sim Cotton's most potent enemy; that time passing with the control of the town in doubt was like a cancer gnawing at his vitals. Those awaiting his next move could scarcely know that the loss of Norris and Rodgers had robbed him of two of his top guns, or that the beating Art Cotton had taken had stripped layers of pride from Sim Cotton himself, leaving nerves seared and screaming for revenge. But he was in control. He rode down the street like a king, tall and proud, a big man, virile and confident. He reined his horse to a stop in front of the Oasis and was about to dismount when a cold voice rasped, 'Don't get down.'

He settled back in his saddle. A small pulse started to beat in his forehead, the slow measured beat of building rage; but no trace of it appeared on his face.

'I've ridden a long way,' he said mildly. 'I'd like a drink.'

'Drink someplace else,' snapped another voice. 'Saloon's shut – to yu.' Sim Cotton's eyes moved to meet those of the speaker, the bartender, Blass.

'Well, Blass,' he said, a touch of iciness in his voice, 'I hope yu've thought what yo're doin' though.'

'First real thinkin' I've done in years,' snapped Blass. 'An' the saloon's still shut.'

Cotton shrugged, dismissing the bartender, and returned his reptilian gaze to Sudden.

'So yu came back,' he said softly. He surveyed the puncher from head to foot. 'Yu don't look good enough to have beaten Art.' His lip curled contemptuously. 'Yu don't look much at all.'

'Take another look at yore brother,' Sudden told him flatly. 'O' course, he might'a just fell on his face.' A cold smile lit his eyes for a moment. 'Howdy, Helm. Yore head better?' He might have been asking an old-timer about his rheumatism. Helm cursed and his hand moved, but Cotton stopped him with a word.

'No gunplay!' he snapped. 'I ain't come here to fight.'

'Be interestin' to know why yu did come,' suggested Sudden, but his voice lacked any sign of interest.

'Oh . . .' Cotton pursed his lips. 'A talk. An exchange of views. An arrangement, maybe.'

'Such as?'

'Yo're a good man, if yu licked Art an' sent Helm packin'. I can use good men. It's that simple. I thought we could discuss. . . .'

'Yu thought wrong!' Sudden's voice was flat and final, and for a moment cold anger exhibited itself in his mien. 'Yu may be a big man, Cotton, but yo're a long way off the trail. Mebbe yu own a big ranch an' run a hard crew, an' mebbe yu pay 'em well for doin' what yu tell 'em to do. Mebbe that makes a lot o' people do things they don't like doin,' but it don't make yu God, mister. Yore fat-faced sheriff aimed to have me Pecossed, an' I'm guessin' yore man Helm wasn't plannin' on no picnic with the kid, here, when he planned to ride along with him to Santa Fé. Yo're outside the fence, Cotton. Yu got to be put down like a wild animal. No talk, no deal, no nothin'!'

Helm laughed into the chilled silence. 'He talks awful big for a man in such a tight. Look at him! What's he got to buck us with? A kid, a barkeep, a grocer an' a cripple. Hell, I could take all of 'em with one hand tied—'

'Yu want to try it now?'

Sudden's eyes had narrowed to slits and he faced Helm squarely, his body falling into a menacing half-crouch, his very stance instinct with a deadly menace that sent a shiver into the veins of every man watching.

Helm laughed again. 'Hell, I'll take yu any time I want to, Green,' he sneered. 'But my way, not yores.'

'In the back, yu mean?' was the cutting reply.

'Now, see here, Green,' interposed Cotton, 'I come here in good faith—'

'Yu came here to see what was happenin',' jibed the puncher, 'an' now yu know what yo're up against. Yu don't own this town any more, Cotton. We aim to stay here until the US Marshal arrives.' This remark hit Sim Cotton harder than anything said so far. Was the man bluffing, or had he really sent for the Federals? If he had, then the game was getting out of hand. Even Sim Cotton wasn't big enough to tangle with the United States Government – not yet, anyway, he told his pride. Something of what was passing through his mind must have communicated itself to the saturnine figure on the porch of the Oasis, for Cotton saw that Sudden was smiling – a wintry smile, but a smile nonetheless.

'That's right, Cotton, yu better think careful,' Sudden warned the rancher. 'Yu can't buck a US Marshal.'

'I can damned well buck yu, though!' Cotton's mien changed. Blood darkened his visage, and the veins stood out upon his throat and brow. 'Yu better get out o' this town. Yu better ride far an' fast, because I'm comin' back here, an' I'm takin' this town. I'm takin' it an' if yore still here I'm goin' to hang yu in the street an' leave yu there to rot, yu an' these sniv-ellin' backbiters who've sided with yu! Cottons built this place

74

an' by the Eternal! Cottons can unbuild it! I'll burn down every home, every buildin'! I'll line up every snivellin' cur in the place an' shoot him down – the man don't live that can cross me an' tell the tale!' Spittle flecked his lips, and madness made his eyes roll white. The man was wild, far gone out of reach, uncontrollable and murderous. Sudden snapped him back with a cutting query.

'Yu through?'

Cotton's eyes cleared. He blinked once or twice, as if unsure of where he was. Only the gloved hand, closing and unclosing incessantly upon the saddle pommel, indicated the struggle for control that the man was exercising. Cotton took a deep breath.

'No, Green,' he said, his voice still thick with rage, but quietly now, and correspondingly more threatening. 'I ain't through – I ain't even begun yet. But I will. Yu want war? Yu shall have it. The truce is over. Yu'll die afore sundown!'

He jerked the horse's head around and spurring the animal wickedly, thundered off up the street, pursued by his foreman. Harry Parris stood uncertainly in the middle of the street, dust drifting down on him, looking after Cotton and patently wondering what to do – whether to mount and follow Cotton, or remain in the town.

He looked pleadingly at Sudden and the others. They returned his gaze expressionlessly, then turned and walked into the Oasis without a word. Parris stood there for a long time before he shuffled off towards his cabin.

Blass watched him go through his window.

'There goes a worried *hombre*,' he told the silent group who stood by the bar.

'Hell,' said Billy with a nervous laugh. '*He's* worried?'

Sudden smiled, feigning a confidence he was far from feeling.

'Wal,' he drawled. 'He had a better job than we did.' But their laughter had no heart in it.

CHAPTER ELEVEN

Cottontown had a still and empty air. Most of the men in town, after the maniacal threats of Sim Cotton, had taken Sudden's advice and locked their womenfolk and children securely in their homes. For perhaps an hour there had been a tremendous bustle of activity on the curving street, but now all was silent. Billy Hornby's lip curled derisively as he surveyed the deserted street. 'This shore is a yaller-bellied town,' he sneered. 'Damme if I know whether she's worth fightin' for.'

'That ain't why yo're fightin',' Sudden reminded him. 'Don't go judgin' these folks too hard. They ain't been pushed the way yu have; an' none o' them's any kind o' hand with a gun, I'd guess. I'm willin' to bet most of 'em don't fire one from one month to the next. Yu can't expect them to stick their heads into this kind o' fracas.'

A thin silence ensued, a weird, unnatural stillness unbroken by the everyday sounds of children playing, women gossiping in the street, horses and wagons passing outside. Over the town hung an almost tangible apprehension, while men watched from their doorways or through windows, their eyes fixed on the road entering town from the north. To the north lay the Cotton ranch. It was from the north they would come. Sudden had made his plans. Now he deployed his forces.

'Billy,' he told the youngster. 'I want yu to sneak out mebbe half a mile from town along the trail towards the Cotton spread. Take a water canteen. Stash yoreself in the rocks someplace where yu can see the trail without bein' seen. As soon as yu spot riders comin', duck out o' sight. Let 'em pass, yu hear? Don't try to stop 'em, whatever yu do. Just let 'em come in.

76

When they're well past, pull yore gun an' fire her three times in the air, fast. That'll be our warnin' that they're on their way in.'

Billy's expression was crestfallen. Then it brightened.

'Listen, Jim, why don't I take a rifle out with me? I could pick 'em off afore they get into town.'

Sudden looked at his young friend in mild exasperation, then asked Doc Hight a question.

'How many men can Sim Cotton raise if he needs to?'

Hight considered for a moment, lips pursed.

'Maybe fifteen, if you count Bucky an' Art,' he replied.

'Yu aimin' to take on fifteen men all by yoreself?' Sudden asked the boy. 'Or would yu rather do it my way?'

Billy grinned. 'Okay, okay. I was just tryin' to help.'

'Then do what I tell yu. This ain't no game we're playin. Give us the warnin'. Then skedaddle back into town. That'll give us a man in back o' them if we need one. Come in careful. Don't take no chances. Yu hear me?'

Billy nodded. 'Watch 'em go by. Fire three shots. Then follow 'em in not too close, slow an' careful. Hell, Jim yu could train a monkey to do that.'

'Then I'm pickin' right,' was the smiling retort. 'Git movin'.'

When the boy had gone, Sudden turned to the remaining three men and gave them their dispositions. The bartender and storekeeper he told to take up positions on the flat roof of the saloon behind the tall false front.

'Yu'll be well hid,' he told them. 'Don't show yore faces until the waltz begins. As soon as yu've done shootin' get down out o' there. Once yo're spotted, that'll be somewhere yu don't want to stay.' Blass and Davis nodded, and the latter purposefully levered his Winchester.

'By the Eternal!' he growled. 'I hope they do start somethin'. I shore owe them boys a lick or two.'

'Don't be too eager,' Sudden counselled him. 'Wait for me to start the ball. An' yu, Doc: I want you over in the sheriff's house. Keep an eye on him, make shore he don't give us no trouble. If yu got to, tap him one with yore gunbarrel.'

'Where will you be, Jim?' asked the medico.

'Me?' said Sudden with mock surprise. 'Why, I'll be over by the jail, mindin' my own business.'

'Yo're goin' to make yoreself the bait?' gasped Blass.

'Yu might say that,' Sudden told him, his face sobering. 'I'm relyin' on yu boys to see I don't get et.'

'Yu reckon Sim is goin' to rush the town, Jim?' asked Davis.

'He never said,' Sudden grinned. 'But I reckon not. Cotton knows he's on the wrong side o' the law now. He got mighty edgy when I mentioned the US Marshal. If he thinks he might have to explain what happened later on, he's going to make it look as right as he can. That don't include no massacree.'

'Was you serious about havin' sent for the Marshal, Jim?' Hight said. 'I don't recall. . . .'

'Just a bluff,' Sudden replied. 'Like I said, Cotton's on the wrong side o' the law, an' he might just fall over an' break his neck tryin' to make it look like he's on the right side.' He walked over to the window, and peered out into the street.

'All quiet,' he announced. 'Try an' get to yore posts without attractin' too much attention. It would be a shame to spoil the surprise.' His thin smile boded ill for the men who were to be the recipients of this surprise.

While his companions hastened to their positions, Sudden crossed the street to the jail. He sat there on a rock-backed chair, tilted against the wall, his hat pushed forward over his eyes. Beneath the shaded brim, however, the keen gaze missed no movement on the street.

'Shore hope I'm figgerin' that Cotton jasper,' he soliloquised. 'If he hits this town hard, we're goin' to know we've been in a fight.' And saying this his gaze wandered to the unguarded southern end of the town, and the line of dusty green which marked the banks of the river. His mind was busy. 'If I was Sim Cotton, how would I play her?' he asked himself. 'What would I expect me to think I'd do?' The nonsensical character of his question brought a smile to his lips. After sitting for a while deep in thought, he stepped out into the street, pacing purposefully. A quick glance showed him that Blass was in position, and a moment later he glimpsed the storekeeper on the opposite side of the false front of the salon, their rifles commanding the whole length of the street. Sudden glanced now towards the sheriff's small shack. Hight waved from behind the closed window, a quick signal that all was well. Sudden nodded.

'Well, we're all set to go to the ball. All we need now is the music.'

He walked back towards the jail and leaned casually against the porch rail, relaxed and waiting.

Up on the saloon roof the bartender shook his head.

'Look at him,' he told his companion. 'Yu'd think he had nothin' more on his mind than the next drink! That jasper ain't got no nerves!'

Davis grinned and said, 'Wal, it's probably just as well. I reckon we got enough for us an' some left over for him.'

Blass shook his head wonderingly. 'He shore is a cool sort o' cucumber. I'll tell yu one thing: he ain't no ordinary forty an' found cowpoke.'

'Yu ain't whistlin' Dixie,' agreed the storekeeper. 'I still ain't figgered out why he ain't skedaddled. This yere fight ain't none of his never-mind. I'd say he done considerable more than he needed to when he bruk the kid out o' jail. Why for yu reckon he's pitchin' in this hoedown?'

Blass shrugged. 'No good reason I can see,' he said. 'Unless he just enjoys a scrap.'

'He better had,' was the rejoinder. 'For we're shore as hell in for one.'

With this remark silence fell between them, and they turned their eyes towards the street, empty and yawning below them, except for the motionless figure of James Green, standing alone and waiting.

Chris Helm smiled like a wolf as the three shots rang out behind him.

'Sim was right,' he told the three men with him.

'Figgered,' agreed the villainous-looking half breed on his right. 'They must have us down as pretty stupid if they reckon we're goin' to ride into a whipsaw.'

'I don't reckon they know what to expect,' Helm told him. 'That's why we're playin' it the way I told yu afore we left the ranch.'

'Yu reckon yu can drag it out until we get around?' asked a short, narrow-eyed man wearing his gun on the left side, butt forward.

'Yu just get there, Hitch,' Helm said. 'An' come in fast when I take Green.'

'Yu sound awful shore he'll come out after yu alone,' Hitch argued.

'I am,' was the unemotional reply. 'Who else could he send?'

The quartet reined in their horses. Over a rise perhaps a hundred yards in front of them the town could be clearly seen, spread unprettily across the grey-green prairie like toy houses dropped by a tired child. Beyond and to the southwest the thin line of trees marking the curve of the river laid a strip of brighter colour across the land.

'Yu boys got it straight, now?' Helm asked, harshly. 'I don't want no slip-ups. When yu see me set him up, yu come up that street *fast*! Felipe, yu take the saloon side. Bann, yu take the middle. I want yu on the jailhouse side, Hitch. Keep yore eyes on the roofs, all o' yu. They may have more men than we figger. Okay, move out!'

The three Cottonwood riders thundered off at a tangent across the area between the town and the river. Helm drew his guns, spun the cylinders, checked the action, and thrust them back into the tooled leather holsters. He slapped his horse into motion and moved slowly ahead towards the northern end of the town.

The three shots rang out, flat and emphatic, in the open prairie beyond the northern edge of town The two men on the roof saw Sudden straighten up and step slowly forward into the centre of the street. They scanned the northern end of the street, and presently the lone horseman moving in a leisurely fashion towards the edge of town.

'One man alone,' frowned Davis. 'Are they mad?'

'Mebbe, mebbe not,' was the terse reply. 'Keep yore sights on him regardless. Jim,' he called. 'One man. Looks like the big feller, Helm.'

'Nobody else in sight, no dust?' called the man in the street without taking his eyes off the rider now visible at the far end of town.

'Nary a thing,' came the reply.

Sudden nodded and gestured them to conceal themselves again. He watched as the lone rider dismounted outside the general store and tied up his horse. Helm looked as if he were no more concerned than if he were really going into the store for some tobacco as Sudden paced slowly forward, up the street past the saloon now and drawing level with the bank.

Helm stepped away from his horse's side into the middle of the street, perhaps fifty yards away from the approaching Sudden. He smiled thinly, settling on his heels, letting Sudden come to him.

'Keep comin', cowboy,' he said softly to himself. 'Keep comin'.' Aloud, he called, 'Yu got any last words for yore tombstone, Green?'

Sudden stopped, measuring the man. Helm's confidence was no real surprise, for the man was a professional gunfighter, had been through this before so many times that it must almost be a ritual by now. Sudden's mouth went grim as he thought of the men, innocent men, unskilled in the use of guns, who had fallen dead at this killer's feet.

'Yeah,' Sudden told him, stopping about twenty feet away from the gunfighter. 'Yu might make shore they put *alias Sudden* on it.' Consternation touched Helm's face for a moment, but then confidence reasserted itself.

'So yo're Sudden,' he sneered. 'I thought I knew yu. They say yo're fast.'

Sudden noted that for a fraction of a second, Helm's eyes were focused on some distant point behind him down the street, but his cold gaze did not leave the man before him.

'Yu got the choice o' findin' out or gettin' out, Helm,' Sudden told him. 'Make it.'

'In my own time, Mister Sudden,' Helm smiled. He was

almost relaxed, only the cat eyes wary and watchful. 'I'll take yu when I'm good an' ready.'

The two men stood for a frozen second, as if time itself was standing still. Then a door banged open and in that same moment, all hell broke loose on the street of Cottontown.

CHAPTER TWELVE

Doc Hight had watched Sheriff Parris like a hawk from the moment he heard the three warning shots echo flatly across the town. The old man had given him no trouble, but had remained where Doc had told him to stay, flat against the far wall of the shack, his hands behind his neck.

In the suspenseful moments following Helm's arrival in town, which Hight could not see, Parris played on the medico's taut nerve with telling comments.

'Yore sidekicks will run out on yu, Doc,' he cackled, evilly. 'Yo're goin' to look mighty sick when Sim Cotton's boys get yu.'

'Keep your mouth shut,' rapped Hight. 'I might just take Green's advice and tap you one with this.' He gestured with the gun barrel. The sheriff was unabashed by this threat, however.

'Yu lay into me, an' yu'll get twice yore value when Sim's done with yu, boy,' he jibed. 'Yu better turn me loose while yu got a chance.'

'I'll put a bullet in your fat belly if you don't keep still,' growled Hight, now uncertain as the continuing stillness outside remained unbroken. Where was Green? What was happening? He edged over towards the window, peered out, looking up the street. He saw Green walking slowly north towards something or someone he couldn't see. He pushed his face harder against the glass, trying to bring the far end of the street within his range of vision. In this moment, his attention was completely diverted from the old sheriff, who, with an agility surprising in a man so large, took three fast steps across the room and crashed a clenched fist to the base of the medico's neck. Hight dropped, stunned, to his knees as the sheriff wrenched the pistol from his nerveless fingers. The gun rose high and fell, stretching Hight unconscious on the floor.

Without further thought, Parris rushed across the room and pulled open the door which led directly on to the street, yelling at the top of his voice 'On the saloon roof, boys! Watch out on the—' and that was all he ever said for the precise moment that he wrenched open his front door and dashed out into the street, the three Cottonwood riders who had circled the town came out at full gallop from behind the jail, guns drawn, bearing down on the lone figure of Sudden in the street.

Felipe, the half breed screamed aloud as his horse ran straight into the sheriff. In another second the three riders were fighting their panic-stricken horses, trying desperately to stay in the saddle, as the guns started to boom.

Helm's hands had flashed for his guns in the moment he heard the door bang, sure that the sound of his comrades approaching would momentarily distract the calm, saturnine figure before him. Helm was very, very fast. He had moved before Sudden even started for his guns, and Helm had his fingers crooked on the triggers when twin spurts of flame belched from Sudden's hips, hurling Helm backwards and over, the gunman's guns exploding as the reflex action made him jerk the triggers. Helm died happy thinking he had killed Sudden, while Sudden, moving even as the shots he had fired whisked Helm over, was rolling sideways and turning, his twin revolvers blasting shots into the twisting, churning mass that was the three riders in the street. One horse was down hurt, and the others were still rearing, screeching as the bullets whined about them and the roll of gunfire multiplied the panic caused by the moving thing that had tangled itself in their legs. The half-breed, Felipe, lay cursing, one leg twisted at an unnatural angle, sidling towards the revolver which lay in the dust. Blass and Davis stood up on the saloon roof, pouring rifle fire into the struggling group in the street. The dust rose high and figures became obscure. Still the two men on the roof kept firing, and went on shooting until their weapons were empty.

The silence when the firing ceased was shattering. Sudden edged along the saloon porch, guns cocked and ready, as the dust sifted down in the street and figures became distinct again. One horse was dead, its body half covering the tattered, smashed thing that had once been the sheriff. The other horses had skittered off down the street until their dragging reins had halted them; they stood now, nervously snorting and pawing the dust, just beyond the jail. The three Cottonwood riders were dead. None of them had fired a shot.

Sudden was standing in the middle of the street looking down at the carnage when the bartender and the storekeeper joined him.

'My Gawd!' gasped Blass in an awed voice. 'Did we do that?'

'I just kept shootin',' Davis said, 'I couldn't see nothin', but I kept shootin'.'

'It's over now,' Sudden told them. He felt a great weariness for a moment. 'Go an' see what happened to Doc Hight. He may be hurt.'

The two men hurried off towards the sheriff's cabin. Looking up Green saw Billy Hornby running down the street, as men emerged from doorways, their actions curiously hesitant.

'Jim!' Billy called. 'I stayed up at the north end, in case they come runnin' back that way. I didn't know they'd split up. Is any one hurt?'

'On'y them,' the puncher told him. 'We come out without a scratch.'

'I see yu got Helm,' Billy enthused. 'Good for yu.'

'He had it comin',' Green said flatly. 'But I ain't proud of it. I ain't proud of any o' this. If Harry Parris hadn't taken it into his head to try an' let Helm know somethin' Helm knew already, it'd be us lyin' there.'

He looked around as the two men came out of Parris's house with Doc Hight. The medico was rubbing his head; his face was a picture of chagrin.

'Jim,' he began. 'I'm shore sorry. . . .'

'Forget it,' Sudden retorted. 'In a way, yu helped. Those three woulda given me a bad moment if it hadn'ta been for Parris.'

He glanced over towards the Oasis. 'I reckon I could use a drink,' he announced, and without another word strode purposefully across the street, while his four allies watched him with amazed expressions.

Billy Hornby broke the silence. 'Chris Helm in front o' him an' three paid guns ridin' him down from behind, an' he allows they might've given him a *bad moment*.' He shook his head. 'Gents, I aim to take a drink with a *man* – the first real man to hit this town in a long time.'

He followed Sudden towards the saloon. After a moment, Hight looked at the other two.

'Damned if he ain't right,' he told them.

CHAPTER THIRTEEN

Sim Cotton was worried. He was not normally a worrying man, but the events of the past half-dozen hours had played havoc with his carefully-wrought plans. Not for the first time, he silently cursed the rebel boy who had precipitated this debacle and the brother whose thoughtless, stupid act had started it all. Twenty minutes before, a startled shout had brought him to his feet in the big room of the Cottonwood ranch, and he had gone outside to see one of his riders running towards the house, a piece of paper clutched in his hand.

'It was Helm's hoss,' the man gasped. 'An' this was pinned on to the saddle.' He handed the note to his employer.

Cotton snatched the paper out of the man's hand and read it. It was brief and to the point.

'Your move' he read. He crumpled the paper into a ball and hurled it to the ground. 'Damn the man! He musta got Helm! But how? There wasn't a man in this territory fast enough to beat Chris.'

'Mebbe they bushwhacked him,' suggested the rider.

'Get back to yore work!' snapped Cotton, turning and stamping back into the house. He hurled himself into an armchair and lit a black cigar, clamping his teeth into it and smoking furiously, his brows knit. What had happened in Cottontown? How many men had this Green rallied around him? Had Helm been ambushed? If so, how had the plan they had concocted fared? What was Parris doing? He recalled the remark the cowpuncher had made about a US Marshal. Had Green been bluffing? Or was the Federal lawman on his way? If so, he would arrive within the next twenty four hours. Sim

Cotton got to his feet, paced forward and back across the stone floor of the Cottonwood ranch house living room. He was still pacing when his brother came in, having been told of the news.

'Sim!' Art's disbelieving voice stopped his brother in mid-stride. 'They didn't get Helm?'

Sim looked at Art, saying nothing, just looking at him.

Art's stare fell, and he slumped into a chair. 'My Gawd!' he breathed.

'Who *is* this feller Green?'

'He ain't no driftin' cowboy, that's for shore,' muttered Buck Cotton.

'I don't care if he's Abraham Lincoln!' snapped Sim Cotton. 'We got to root him out o' there. As long as he's alive, we ain't controllin' Cottontown, an' if we ain't controlling Cottontown then we ain't controlling anythin' in these parts. They'll build that dam, parcel out the land to nesters, an' we'll be left with the land this ranch stands on an' not one lousy acre more. We'll be bust flat, an' I ain't sittin' here lettin' that happen.' Art looked up at his brother, his lacklustre eyes shining with interest from beneath his puffed, bruised brows.

'What yu aimin' to do, Sim?' he asked.

'Do we ride in an' wipe 'em out?' added Buck eagerly.

'Shore,' the older man agreed with massive scorn. 'That's real bright thinkin'. That's makin' it easy for them. We all ride in nice an' bunched, an' they lay for us on the rooftops. They'd cut us to pieces afore we got past the bank. If we ride into that town, we got to stay there. The question is: was that puncher bluffin' about the US Marshal?'

'He shore don't give the impression o' bein' much on bluff,' said Buck. 'As Art here can testify.' He flinched as his brother laid a glowering glance of hatred upon him. The beating he had taken at Green's hands had left deep scars on Art Cotton, and not all of them showed.

'Hell's teeth!' cursed Sim Cotton. Everything had been doing so well. His influence in the town had been unassailable. All had been ready for the final coup – and now, this. What was the answer?

88

'We got to go in,' he decided finally. 'We got to take that town back.' He smashed his fist into his palm. 'There's too much at stake to back out now. We got to take that town. An' I want to watch that drifter dance at the end of a rope!'

Art Cotton rose to his feet.

'Now yo're talkin', Sim!' he enthused. 'We'll roll them tenderfeet up like a carpet!'

'No!' Sim Cotton thundered. 'We play our cards very careful. We filter into town quiet-like. No noise. Take over the place. Pull in a man, two men. First thing we got to do is find out how many men Green's got with him, afore we make our move.' His face was now suffused with a look of pure animal cunning. He turned to his younger brother.

'Now, Bucky, yu get yore chance to do somethin' towards puttin' this mess right. Yu better do it properly. I won't give yu no second chance, yu hear?'

Buck Cotton nodded eagerly, his face white, anxious to please this frowning man who seemed suddenly to be a deadly stranger and not his forgiving older brother. 'Shore Sim,' he managed. 'Just name it, an' it's done.'

Sim Cotton nodded. 'They got the town. We want it. But we ain't got anythin' to offer them for it. Now Bucky here knows where there's somethin' that'll bring that nester kid out into the open like a bee-stung porkypine . . .' he grinned evilly. 'Yu followin' me, Bucky?'

The younger man's face was puzzled for a moment, and then understanding dawned, bringing a wolf-like grin to his features.

'The girl!' he breathed. 'O' course. They'll come out like sheep if we got the girl! Sim, yo're a genius! Why didn't I think o' that?

'I wonder,' Art said sourly, his lip curled.

'Yu boys ain't got time for this kid scrappin',' snapped Sim. 'Bucky, get on yore way. Bring the gal to Mott's house. That's where we'll be. An' don't make no slips, boy. Mind me, now! Don't make no slips, or yo're finished!'

Buck Cotton nodded, chastened out of his delight at Sim's idea of kidnapping the Hornby girl. He slammed out of the house and saddled up his horse, muttering to himself.

'Shore must think I'm dumb,' he mumbled. 'I'll show him. When he's got this town in his paw again, he better remember me.' He leapt into the saddle and spurred off across the scrubland, heading southeast towards the Lazy H, and as he rode he thought again about the girl, and as he thought about her his eyes shone wildly.

CHAPTER FOURTEEN

The Lazy H lay in a small hollow, a neat, low-slung stone house of five rooms, L-shaped and compact beneath the shading oak and elm trees watered by the river which burbled by on its course towards the Rio Grande, its banks not fifty yards from the house itself. Buck Cotton pulled his horse to a stop on the top of the slope, and dismounted, scanning the area in front of the house and the corral off on the southern side. There was no sign of a horse, no sign of movement. He nodded to himself, an eager smile playing around his lips.

'Pie like mother made,' he told himself. 'I wonder where the Mex woman is?'

As if in answer to his question a woman emerged from the house carrying a tub full of washing which she hefted towards the pump in the yard, proceeding to energetically splash water upon the clothes in the tub.

Moving cautiously, Buck got to within a few yards of her before the woman looked up with startled eyes into the gaping barrel of Buck's sixgun. Buck had a finger on his lips.

'Don't make a sound,' he hissed, 'or. . . .' He gestured with the gun. '*Comprende?* The woman nodded, her eyes wide with fear. '*A donde es la señorita?*' Buck asked her. 'Where's the girl?'

The woman pointed towards the house. '*En la casa,*' she said.

'She alone?'

Another nod.

'Right! Lead on inside,' he told her, pointing with the gun. '*Vamos!*' Looking fearfully over her shoulder, the woman shuffled towards the door. She went inside, turning sharply right as she did so, and Buck came in smoothly after her, blinking to adjust his eyes to the sudden gloom of the interior. He hardly saw the blur of movement, the chopping descent of the gun-barrel wielded by Billy Hornby which cracked his wrist-bone like a dried twig, slashing the gun from his numb fingers. Buck Cotton's reflexes were good, even so. He tried to move fast out of the way but stumbled backwards out into the sunlit yard, sprawling in the dirt, unable to help break the fall with his injured arm, and looked up to see Billy Hornby standing over him spraddle-legged, the heavy .45 cocked in his hand, only his thumb holding back the hammer, and a terrible fear possessed Buck Cotton. For the look on Hornby's face was one of insane rage. Buck watched for perhaps ten endless seconds as Billy Hornby tried to force himself to release the hammer of the gun and kill the hated thing at his feet, but the boy could not do it. With something like a sigh, Billy's tenseness abated, and the light came back into his eyes. Buck Cotton, sweating on the ground, knew that for the moment he would live. He tried to get up, but Billy lined the gun on him again.

'Stay in the dirt where yu belong, yu sidewinder!' he grated. 'I still ain't shore I didn't ought to salivate yu.'

Buck lay still. Any argument with this fury-filled young man was useless. One wrong move and Billy would kill him.

'Green figgered yu'd try somethin' like this,' Billy told him. 'He said he had some trouble tryin' to think like a rat, but once he got the hang of it, it was easy to guess what yore play'd be. I sent Jenny down to Fort Lane afore all this started, Bucky-boy. Which turns the tables a mite. That's the on'y reason yu ain't buzzard-bait already.'

Buck Cotton frowned up at his captor. 'What yu ravin' about, Hornby?' he said.

'Hell, I knew yu was dumb, Buck, but if yu can't see it. . .!' Billy shook his head. 'I do reckon yu can't, at that. Yu was comin' out here to try to kidnap Jenny an' use her as a hostage, right?'

Cotton shook his head. 'I don't know what yo're talkin' about,' he mumbled.

'Sez yu,' was the impolite retort. 'But now, instead o' Jenny bein' yore brother's ace in the hole, it's the other way round. Yo're ours. It'll be interestin' to see how tough he gets with yu in our hands.'

Fear struck at Buck Cotton's vitals. Sim had warned him that if he failed to bring in the girl, he was finished. Knowing his brother, Buck was well aware that Sim would never bargain – he had said as much at the ranch.

'Yo're crazy!' he cried, hoarsely. 'Sim won't do no deals with yu!'

'We'll have to see about that,' replied Billy grimly. 'Either way yu lose, Cotton. Yu ought to've stayed home with yore head down.'

The other stood up, trembling, his mind a seething mass of wild ideas. How could he break away from this menacing youth and get word to Sim without being killed? Would Sim accept that he had no way of bringing in the girl? A thought occurred to him and he voiced it.

'How was yu so shore we wouldn't all ride over here?' he asked.

'Wasn't,' Billy retorted succinctly. 'If Manuela had seen more'n one man she was goin' to give me the word. She woulda just told yu that Jenny wasn't here. I woulda laid low till yu was gone. As it was, yu come alone. An' now I've got yu, yu sonofabitch, I hope yo're feelin' fit.'

Buck Cotton frowned at this last remark. What had his fitness to do with anything? Seeing his captive's puzzlement, Billy Hornby laughed aloud.

'Yo're wonderin' why I said that?' he grinned. 'Shucks, that's easy, Bucky-boy. Yo're walkin' to town.'

'Walkin'!' Buck Cotton's face was horror-stricken. To have to walk more than fifty feet was something the average Westerner avoided like the plague – he would rather mount a horse to cross the street than cross it on foot. The high heeled boots so practical for the man in the saddle were hardly designed for hiking, and the mere thought of the tramp into town filled Buck Cotton with anguish

'Yu wouldn't . . . yu couldn't make a man walk all that way!' he gasped.

'A man, mebbe not,' was Billy's sardonic retort 'Yu, that's somethin' else. Yu hardly qualify as a man in my books.' He lifted the lariat from Buck's horse, and shook the noose free. This he placed about the Cottonwood man's neck.

'Don't go gettin' any ideas about slidin' off,' Billy warned him. 'Or yo're likely to get that choked-up feelin'.'

He swung into the saddle and shook the rope.

'Start walkin',' he commanded. 'It's a fair stretch to Cottontown.'

Stumbling, cursing, tears of frustrated rage in his eyes, Buck Cotton began his ignominious trek towards town. Behind him easy and watchful in the saddle, Billy Hornby followed the man, his eyes cold and without sympathy. Cotton, for his part, nursed his hatred. Hornby did not know that by the time they reached town Sim and his riders would be moving in on his friends. He might get a bad shock even yet. The thought buoyed him up, kept him moving forward at a shambling walk across the unlovely scrubland southeast of the town.

Bob Davis was guarding the window in the Oasis, his eyes sweeping up and down the empty street, watching for any movement which might indicate hostile action. But the town was empty and still. Even the few men who had emerged from their homes after the fight in the street were nowhere to be seen. 'Gone to ground somewheres,' Davis told himself. 'Can't say I blame 'em. Come to think of it, I wouldn't mind joinin' 'em.' Aloud, he addressed a question to Sudden.

'Yore guess is as good as mine, Bob,' Sudden told him in reply. 'If they rode out to try for the girl, Billy oughta be comin' in hell-for-leather any minnit. Then we'll know where they are. Otherwise, like I said, yore guess is as good as mine.'

'I don't like it,' muttered Doc Hight. 'It's too damn quiet.'

The momentary silence which followed his words was broken then by the soft thud of hoofs approaching, and Sudden was on his feet in one swift surge, moving towards the batwing doors. Blass and the doctor moved quickly to their posts by the other window, and a gasp of surprise escaped the medico's lips.

'It's the kid,' he announced, unbelievingly. 'An' he's got Bucky Cotton in front o' him. Will you *look* at him!'

The captured Cotton was indeed a sight to see. His clothes were covered with white gypsum dust, which had caked his face and been turned in places to mud by sweat or tears or both. His fine soft leather boots were tattered and one of the heels was missing, making him limp heavily. His hair was matted, and his eyes wild; a steady stream of curses mumbled from his dust-caked lips as he weaved about at the end of the rope held by Billy Hornby. The boy moved slowly up the street from the bridge, his eyes wary, gun out. He passed Doc Hight's house and drew level with the jail, half turning his horse towards the saloon and nearly jerking the half-demented Buck Cotton off his feet.

'Blast my eyes!' crowed Blass, 'the kid's shore got his share o' sand. I'll go an' give him a hand!'

Sudden whirled to protest, but the bartender was already through the swing doors and out on the sidewalk, calling to the boy.

'Billy!' he yelled. 'Yu shore—'

He never finished the sentence. A lance of flame blossomed from the jailhouse and then another.

Buck Cotton let out an animal sound, something between a scream and a shout, turning, stumbling to his knees, screeching 'Sim! Sim!' as the men in the saloon blasted a fusillade towards the unseen assassins across the street.

Blass had stopped as if he had run into a wall, and uncertainty made him hesitate for a fatal moment before he tried to turn on his heel and get back towards the saloon. A volley of shots took him off his feet and slammed him face down on the steps of the saloon, even as Billy yanked back on the rope around Buck Cotton's neck, hauling the Cottonwood man backwards on his knees, eyes bugging and face contorted, fighting to breathe, his fingers scrabbling to tear the searing noose from his throat. Billy hauled his horse around as Sudden and his two companions laid down a slashing hail of lead across the windows and doors of the jail. Bullets whined off the adobe walls and for a moment there was a break in the firing from the ambushers. Billy was turned around now, yanking Buck Cotton backwards, half dragging him along the street as the boy tried to head for the cover of the stable. A ragged cheer escaped Doc Hight's throat only to die stillborn as a hail of shots was loosed at Billy. He lurched in the saddle, fighting to stay on top of the horse, and then lurched again and went over the side, ploughing down like a broken doll into the dirt of the street about ten yards from the front of the livery stable.

The panic-stricken horse, however, had not stopped. It sunfished for a moment as its rider slid from its back, then wheeled again, the rope around Buck Cotton's neck looped to the saddle pommel twanging taut.

'Stop that damn hoss!' yelled a voice across the street in the jail, and a man dashed out, throwing himself prone, a rifle levelled at the horse. Sudden's gun spoke and the man's head fell forward, the rifle slipping from limp hands.

This shot brought a shuddering whiny from the terrified horse. Its ears went back and with a scream it lunged forward, stampeding across the street, hurtling through the gap between the jail and the sheriff's house, dragging behind it a lurching, bumping screaming bundle.

'My Gawd!' breathed Davis. 'He never had a chance.'

'He didn't deserve one,' snapped Sudden harshly. 'Cover me! I'm goin' to get the kid.'

Without another word, he vaulted out of the shattered window and had rolled twice, across the sidewalk and into the street, lighting down on all fours, crouched, guns levelled, before Hight and Davis recovered from their astonishment and laid covering fire above his head. Sudden's right hand gun barked twice as he moved fast and erratically, towards where the boy lay. Shots whined about him. One tugged at the sleeve of his shirt, another ruffled his hair. Gouts of dust and sand plunked into the air and still he was not harmed. He reached the boy's side. Billy's back was black with blood, and there was a dark stain beneath his head. A quick glance around revealed to Sudden that several figures were running into the street. He emptied a gun at them and they broke and scattered for buildings and doorways. Without wasting a moment, Sudden picked up the slumped body of Billy Hornby as though the burly youth had been but a child and slung him unceremoniously across his shoulder. Stumbling, half falling, he ran for the door of the livery stable as more shots from the jailhouse whispered by him, and thunked into the wooden walls of the building. Once inside, Sudden laid the boy as gently as he could on to a pile of straw and wheeled to face the doorway, shooting at the running figures across by the jail until the hammer clicked flatly upon an empty chamber. They faded back out of sight and for a moment there was a brief respite. Sudden took advantage of this to push the heavy plank door shut, and then dropped the heavy timber bar into place behind it.

With a glance at the still-unconscious boy, he methodically reloaded his guns, moving across to one of the windows facing the street for a guarded glance outside. The street was empty and still. A frown touched his forehead for a moment. He wondered whether the storekeeper and the doctor had managed to make good their escape. They had agreed earlier that if for any reason their group was split, that the three townsmen would try to escape to Fort Lane. Two, now, Sudden told himself bitterly. Blass had taken three or four bullets, had never known what hit him. He turned at the sound of movement, and found Billy sitting up groggily on the pile of straw. He was touching the bullet burn across his forehead gingerly, unaware of the wound in his chest.

'Jim . . .' he began weakly. 'I had Buck . . . Cotton. Then all hell broke loose.'

'I'm a mite cross with yu, Billy,' Sudden told him severely. 'Yu shore ought to've knowed better than to ride into town as if yu was leadin' a parade. If things wasn't so busy right now, I shore might be tempted to. . . .' He broke off as Billy's smile faded and the boy slid backwards in a dead faint.

With a final brief look at the still empty street, Sudden moved over to the boy's side and stripped off the blood-soaked shirt. The wound in Billy's shoulder was an ugly one. A bullet had drilled a ragged hole through from just above his shoulder blade in the back to below the collar bone in the front. Another had burned a track across his scalp.

'Lost plenty o' blood,' Sudden surmised, 'but it didn't hit bone. He's a lucky boy. Half an inch lower down an' him and Buck Cotton'd be meetin' up again.'

He took the shirt over to where the water barrel stood by the horse stalls, washing it out thoroughly and then tearing it into wide strips. From these he made a rough compress and bandage, and then scouted about the dusty sable for a moment or two, returning with a handful of cobwebs from a corner.

'Injun medicine's the on'y kind I savvy, Billy,' he told the inert figure. 'I'm shore hopin' that ol' Piute knowed what he was talkin' about!' He pressed the cobwebs against the wound and then laid the wet compress over them. He wiped away the rest of the blood, and repeated the operation at the back where the bullet had entered. He then bound the boy's shoulder as well as he could so that the boy's arm was held close against his chest. If he moved while he was unconscious he wouldn't start the bleeding again.

'Well, I hope it holds yu, kid,' Sudden muttered. 'Now: how do we get out o' this place?'

He cast his eyes hopefully about the stable. It was more or less square shaped, a one-storey edifice of timber with a peaked roof below which heavy timber rafters ran parallel to form a sort of false ceiling. From these hung saddles and bridles, harness, and tools. Sudden wondered idly where the hostler was. 'Run for the ol' Fort, more'n likely,' he guessed. The side walls had no windows in them, and the back of the stable was equipped only with a small, heavily-barred door and a tiny window which was, he noted with satisfaction, barred and shuttered. The huge front doors, wide enough when swung back to admit a wagon and team, were flanked by larger windows, both of which were already shattered and splintered by the hail of bullets which had followed Sudden's rescue dash. Huge slivers of wood had been driven through the heavy doors by Cotton's men's bullets.

'Time to take another gander,' Sudden informed nobody in

particular, and edged over towards the shattered window. Taking his hat from his head he poked it forward on the end of his gunbarrel until it could be clearly seen from outside. A tremendous fusillade of shots burst out, snatching the hat off the gunbarrel, chopping pieces of wood from the window frame, and chunking into the walls.

Sudden shook his head. 'Never liked that hat, anyhow,' he said. He was worried about the two men who had been brave enough to stand up against the Cotton crew with him. They were alone. Maybe even now, Sim Cotton's men were outflanking the saloon, ready to shoot down like a mad dog anything that moved inside. The puncher cursed aloud.

'Damned if I help 'em an' damned if I don't,' he said. 'No shootin' goin' on . . . so somethin' must be brewin'. But what?'

As if in answer to his question, someone rapped urgently on the rear door. Gun cocked, Sudden slid over towards it.

CHAPTER FIFTEEN

It was Doc Hight. Behind him, Bob Davis stood, his eyes sweeping the bare plot behind the stable, gun cocked and ready to deal with any movement, any threat. Hight's face fell as he saw Sudden's levelled revolver.

'Hell, Jim, don't shoot!' he managed.

'I shore wasn't expectin' company,' Sudden told him. 'How did yu get here without bein' spotted?'

'We built us a little fire in the saloon,' Davis explained. 'Throwed a few cart'idges into it, then skedaddled out the back way. Them Cotton boys out in the street ducked for cover again when the bullets exploded; and then they poured it in again, thinkin' there was still someone there.'

'By which time we was in the arroyo that runs in back o' here,' Hight continued. 'An' here we are. How's the boy?'

'Yu better see for yoreself,' Sudden told him, still smiling at the ingenious method of escape the two men had used.

Hight crossed the stable and knelt down beside the youngster. Billy opened his eyes briefly and managed a grin.

'Hi, Doc,' he whispered. 'Shore sorry to bring yu out on a night like this.'

'Save your strength, son,' Hight advised him. 'You can do your joking when I'm through with you.'

He peeled the compress expertly from Billy's shoulder. An exclamation escaped his lips which brought Sudden and Davis quickly over.

'What in the name of Hades did you put on this wound, Jim?' asked the doctor. 'It looks like mud.'

'Cobwebs,' explained Sudden. 'Old Injun remedy. On'y

thing I could think of.'

'Wal, it might be all right for old Injuns,' allowed Hight, 'but don't be offended if I wash it off and disinfect it, will you?'

Sudden shook his head. 'Yo're the doctor,' he smiled disarmingly.

'I'm not so shore, now that I look closer,' mumbled Hight, his fingers gently probing the wound. 'Those cobwebs have shore stopped the bleeding. You're a lucky young man,' he told Billy. 'Let's see . . . no bones broken. Loss of blood. Shock. You ought to be as right as rain in about a week, ten days.'

'Allus supposin' Sim Cotton don't decide to finish off what he started,' pointed out Davis. He was standing by the window, keeping an eye on the empty street.

'Hold still now,' Hight advised Billy. 'This is the part that nobody likes.' He poured some fluid from a bottle he had taken from his pocket on to a cloth, soaking it. He then slapped the cloth swiftly on to the wound. Billy's face drained of what little colour was left in it, although he allowed no sound to escape his clenched lips.

'Hell . . . Doc . . .' he gritted eventually. 'Wh . . . what was that? Sheep dip?'

'Alcohol,' was the smiling reply.

Billy shook his head. 'I reckon that's takin' a drink the hard way.'

Hight bound the wound up again, and fashioned a sling from the youngster's bandanna.

'Keep that arm as still as you can,' he warned Billy. 'You'll start the bleeding again if you jump around too much.'

'Hell, Doc,' protested the boy. 'If I don't jump around some, I'm likely to get perforated again! An' I shore can't shoot left-handed.'

'Yu'll never have a better chance to learn,' interposed Sudden. He nodded towards the street from his position to the side of the window. Hight and the boy sidled over to join him.

'What's going on?' asked the medico.

'I can't make it out,' Davis said. 'Hammerin'? What would they be hammerin' on?'

Glancing outside, the doctor saw a group of men at the far

end of the street, well beyond effective pistol range, clustered around something which he could not see. The sound of hammering carried clearly on the silent air.

Billy narrowed his eyes, straining to see what it was that they were doing. 'It . . . it looks like some kind o' table,' he offered.

'O' course!' breathed Sudden. He moved away from the window. 'Bob, Doc, Billy, keep that street covered the whole time. Don't take yore eyes of it. An' Billy – yu give me a runnin' account o' what's goin' on.'

Sudden rummaged about at the back of the stable, eventually finding what he was looking for, a short, wicked-looking leather knife. He snapped the blade off this, and laid it on one side. The thin clink of the breaking steel caused Billy to glance around.

'What yu up to, Jim?' he asked.

'Keep yore eyes on that street,' Sudden told him. 'What's happenin' out there?'

'Looks like they've finished hammerin',' was the reply. 'They're pickin' up the table, or whatever it is. Movin' back o' the store.'

'They'll be headin' for the rear o' the jail. Throw a couple of shots at them if they show theirselves, but don't waste no bullets!'

Sudden was hacking away at the willow slats which woven together formed the separating walls for the horse stalls in the stable. He found one almost six feet in length, and pulled this out, then a thinner, smaller one.

Billy, unable to contain his curiosity, took another peek at his friend's activities.

'What in tarnation? . . . Yu aimin' to fight 'em off with sticks,' Jim?'

Sudden smiled, without once stopping what he was doing, paring the bark away from the smaller shaft. 'Yu may just be right.'

Billy shrugged, and looked at Hight and Davis with his eyebrows raised. Hight shrugged by way of reply. 'Beats me, too,' Davis said. In that moment, several of the Cottonwood riders scuttled across the open space separating the jail and the sheriff's house. Hight threw one quick shot at them without effect. It drew no return fire.

'They're behind the jail, Jim,' Billy called. 'They're gettin' ready.'

'So'm I,' was the uninformative reply. Hight turned now, and saw Sudden busily pouring a stream of gunpowder out of a dozen cartridge cases from which he had extracted the slugs. There was already a small black pile of it on a piece of waxed paper that lay on the floor. What in the name of the devil was the man up to?

'They're shapin' up for somethin', Jim,' called Billy.

'Tell me what's happenin'.'

'They're pushin' somethin' out – it looks like one o' the tables from the saloon. Looks heavy. It ain't movin' easy. Got two men pushin', I'd say.'

'It'll be heavy enough,' Sudden said. 'It's an ol' trick. Yu nail three tabletops together, use them as a shield. Ain't many guns can put a slug through three inches o' timber. Tell me how far they've got.'

'About level with the front o' the jail. They're findin' it hard work. She's stickin' in the sand a mite more'n somewhat.'

'Give 'em a couple of shots,' called Sudden. 'See what happens.' Billy nodded to the doctor, and levelled the gun in his left hand. His shot whined off target, kicking up a gout of sand perhaps six feet to the left of the moving wooden shield.

'Damn!' he exploded. 'I ain't even likely to hit New Mexico shootin' left handed.'

'Rest yore gun on the windowsill,' Sudden called. 'Squeeze yore shots off, gentle-like!'

Billy did as he was told, and this time his shot thwacked into the table-shield, which was now perhaps a quarter of the way across the street. Hight put another two shots into it. Slivers of wood whirred away into the air, but the bullets obviously had not penetrated. The shield continued to make inexorable forward progress, propelled by the men behind it. A veritable barrage of shots exploded from the jail and to the rear of the late Sheriff Parris's house, forcing the men at the windows to duck hastily below the level of the sills. Bullets whined through the gaping window frames, smacking into saddles that were slung on the rafters. One shot hit a metal bit dangling from a hook on the wall, and whisked the bit across the stable with a dissonant jangle of metal. The continuous thunder of shots went on, making it doubly dangerous to look out into the street, and impossible to return the fire. Hight must have dared the former however, for he said tensely, 'They're about half way, Jim!'

'I'm nigh on ready,' was the terse reply. 'Let 'em come a mite nearer.' He was packing the waxed paper parcel into a tack-box which he had found on the blacksmith's workbench. Sudden then straightened up, eyeing the bales of straw stacked against the south wall of the stable. He gauged its height in relationship to the windows and nodded.

'Billy, Doc! Get away from that window!'

The two men moved rapidly away from the window, their widening gaze of astonishment fixed on Sudden. The puncher had fashioned from the willow branches which he had cut from the stalls a makeshift bow and arrow. To the arrow was fastened the tack-box full of powder. Around it was a sheaf of straw. The arrowhead was a broken knife blade.

'What the devil?' exclaimed Hight.

Sudden grinned mirthlessly. 'Yu both better start prayin' this thing works,' he told them. 'I ain't used a bow an' arrow since I was about fifteen. I'm hopin' I recall how it goes. If I get it wrong, I'm begin' yore pardon in advance. We won't be around afterwards if it lands in here.' He clambered up on top of the pile of straw bales.

Billy, unwilling to reveal his ignorance and unable to contain his curiosity, whispered a question to the doctor.

'It's an Injun fire arrow, an' then some,' Hight said. 'Watch!' Sudden struck a match and touched it to the bundle of straw. The flame flickered, then blazed up, and as it did, in one smooth, sweet, sure movement Sudden pulled back the bowstring to its fullest extent and released it.

The burning arrow described a line of light from Sudden's position on top of the bales of straw, thrumming through the window and imbedding itself into the still-advancing wooden shield, low on one side, near the ground.

For perhaps half a second there was a silence, then a thunderous flashing-roar which hurled a cloud of smoke and sand and stones high into the air, spattering the stable walls, pattering down on the roof. Billy thought he had heard a scream but couldn't be sure.

'Put some shots into that smoke!' yelled Sudden. 'Pile it on!' The four of them sent a seeking hail of bullets into the thinning cloud of oily smoke which hung on the afternoon air. Gradually it sifted sideways, swaying in a faint breeze, clearing slowly, thinning, disappearing.

There was a shallow, black-edged hole in the street. The wooden shield lay ten yards away, split into three pieces. Some smaller shards of wood lay scattered about. Between the stable and the still-smoking crater lay two broken, sprawled bodies.

'My Gawd in Heaven!' breathed Davis in an awed voice.

'They never knew what hit them,' commented Hight.

Sudden vaulted down from his platform of straw bales. Outside, the street was still again. Nothing moved. It was as if Cotton's men were stunned by the complete demolition of the wooden shield, by the murderous blast which had torn their two comrades apart. Sudden scanned the street as well as he could without exposing himself to a seeking sniper.

'Where's everybody gone?' he muttered. 'They ought to be hoppin' wild! They ain't that afraid o' four men ... unless. . . .'

'Unless what, Jim?' Billy's question was eager.

'Unless they ain't got many men left themselves!' Sudden told him.

'Let's reckon it up. How many men did yu tell me Sim Cotton had out at the Cottonwood? Fifteen, was it?'

'Somethin' like that,' Billy confirmed.

'Not more?'

'Hell, no. A dozen hardcases was plenty to keep this town in line,' Davis told him with a self-critical smile.

'Yu've proved Cotton wrong about more than that today,' Sudden told him. 'An' if my reckonin's correct, yore Mr Cotton is a mighty worried *hombre*. He ain't a-tall shore whether there's a US Marshal comin' here or not. We know there ain't, but Cotton can't take the chance that I wasn't bluffin'. He's lost some o' his men, includin' his top gun. I'd say, all things bein' equal, that Sim Cotton must be what them novelists call thinkin' furiously.'

'Yeah, shore,' interposed Davis, 'but he ain't exactly short o' manpower. I make it he's still got mebbe seven or eight men left.'

'Odds o' two to one,' muttered Billy. 'We can do it.'

'We can,' Sudden told him grimly, 'as long as we don't use no more ammunition than we got to. I'm pretty low: how about yu men?'

The others checked their cartridge belts quickly, dismay spreading on their faces as they realised how many shots they must have fired during the course of the last few hours.

'Hell's teeth, Jim!' gritted Billy. 'We can't give up now, when we've gone this far. We got to get some more ca'tridges.'

Sudden nodded. 'I know it. Doc – yu got any in yore house?' Hight answered affirmatively, his face setting into serious lines as he realised the import of the puncher's question. He stepped forward and laid a hand on Sudden's arm.

'Oh, no you don't'. he protested. 'You're not going to try to get across there and back for cartridges. You'd get your ears shot off.'

'If I don't get some ammo, they'll be shot off anyways,' was Sudden's laconic reply. 'I'd as lief be shootin' back when it's tried.'

Hight shook his head. 'I've got a better idea,' he announced.' Sudden looked surprised, and the medico continued, 'Think for a minute, Jim. Who knows I'm here? Only Sim Cotton – right?'

Sudden nodded. 'I reckon. Providin' he ain't spread the news.'

'So as long as I can make it across to my house unseen, nobody but him would think it amiss if they saw me in there: right?'

Yu mean, they'd think yu'd been there all the time?' asked Billy.

'Precisely,' said Hight. 'If I slide out of the back door, I can easily get across to my place – you can lay down some covering fire to make them duck down while I'm on open ground – and get the ammunition. Coming back would be the same thing in reverse. And we'd be out of the woods.'

Sudden demurred. 'Hell, doc, I could do that – better than yu, in fact. Just tell me where the slugs are, an' I'll go an' fetch 'em.'

'Jim,' argued Hight patiently. 'You must see the sense of what I've been saying. If any of Cotton's men see me moving around in my own house, that's one thing. If they spotted you, that would be quite another. And once you were cut off, none of us would have much chance. As it is, I'm expendable. You are most decidedly not.'

The other two concurred with this latter statement so vehemently that Sudden was forced to admit the logic of what Hight had said.

'Yo're takin' a big chance, Doc,' he pointed out, relenting.

'Nothing like the chance I'll be taking if I don't go,' Hight told him. 'Now less speeches and more action. Let me get on my way.'

Sudden smiled, the first real smile that had crossed his features all that day. He touched Hight's shoulder.

'Yu'll do,' was all he said, but Hight beamed. Sudden eased the bar from the back door and started to swing it back. The door was open no more than a few inches when a bullet tore into the door-frame, slicing a huge chunk of wood away. The wood went whirring upwards, gashing Hight's cheekbone as Sudden slammed the door back into place and a veritable hail of shots thundered into the door, slapping into the wooden walls, chasing dull echoes around the stable.

'There goes another good idea,' the doctor breathed, mopping away the trickle of blood from his cheek. 'They've got the back covered. Now what, Jim?'

CHAPTER SIXTEEN

Inside the livery stable the beleaguered quartet were holding a council of war. Sudden had been talking steadily, his voice level as he outlined a plan. To the others, it seemed little short of suicidal, and Hight said as much.

'Jim, this is madness!' he gasped. 'I refuse to let you do it.'

'Can yu think of any other way?' was the grim rejoinder.

'Hell, Jim, we don't even know how many men they got out there,' Davis interpolated. 'Yu'd be takin' a mighty big chance . . .'

Sudden's grin was wintry. 'I know it,' he told them. 'I ain't sayin' I'm goin' to enjoy doin' her none. But there ain't no alternative. If we sit here until we run out o' cartridges, they'll overrun us worse'n Crazy Horse hit Custer.'

'How about lettin' me go instead, Jim?' put in Billy.

'Shore,' Sudden said, friendly scorn in his voice. 'Yu'd be fine, shootin' left-handed agin paid guns.'

Billy's face was crestfallen and the puncher clapped him on the shoulder. 'I'm shore grateful for the offer, though,' he told the boy. 'But look at the fac's. If Doc can get to his house, he can grab some cartridges. That'll mean someone's got to keep those jaspers in the front occupied, an' we want plenty o' lead flyin' around their heads if they try to get across the street an' cover their boys. Yu an' Bob can manage that atween yu. Bob shore ain't built for sprintin', an' yu've been winged – which leaves yores truly. Now let's quit arguin' about it an' start some doin'.'

Hight nodded reluctantly. 'Jim's right, boys,' he told them. Davis and the younger man were forced to agree.

'Yu shore yu got it straight, now?' asked Sudden of the medico.

'I reckon,' was Hight's reply. 'Yu slide out and distract these jaspers in the arroyo. As soon as I hear shooting. . . .'

'No matter what it sounds like . . .' Sudden prompted.

'No matter what it sounds like – I make my move and get across to my house.'

'By the time yo're ready to go, I'll be either comin' out o' that arroyo – or not, as the case might be,' Sudden warned him. 'Yu be on yore way afore then. If I don't come out, Bob and Billy'll be makin' their own break after yu. It'll be each man for hisself,' he told them flatly. 'Don't nobody make no fool play on my account.'

The three men nodded miserably in agreement. Hight went on:

'If I get there unseen, I grab some cartridges and get back to the stable whenever I can. That it?'

'That's it,' confirmed Sudden. 'Don't try to get back until it's all clear. I'll be back to cover yu – I hope – an' there won't be no guns on yu from the back. If I ain't – yu'll just have to play her by ear.'

Sudden slid his guns from their holsters in a smooth movement, and carefully checked the action and the loads. He thrust the revolvers back and straightened up. His face was set, and his frame tense with the anticipation of forthcoming action. He knew there was no other way to tackle their desperate situation, but neither was he foolhardy enough to believe that he was not taking a very long chance.

'I'm ready,' he announced. He looked over his shoulder towards Billy Hornby. 'Anyone in sight out there?'

'Not a soul, Jim.'

'Okay. Be ready to cover the street. The minnit anyone shows his mug, blast away at him – it don't matter none whether yu hit anythin' or not. Just discourage 'em from peepin'. Yu ready?'

Billy nodded. He cocked his weapon and laid the barrel along the sill of the window, his slitted eyes sweeping the entire street. At the other window, Davis followed the younger man's example.

'Wal, here goes,' breathed Sudden. 'Don't wait up for me, mother.'

Drawing a deep breath, Sudden stepped swiftly into action, moving in one lithe bound towards the shattered window facing the street. Drawing one gun as he moved, he placed his left hand on the sill and vaulted smoothly out into the street, landing catlike, half-crouched, the cocked gun menacingly aimed ahead. He held this position for perhaps a second, and then straightened, wheeling in the same movement into a swerving run to the left, pounding flat out for the side of the building and the alley between the stable and Doc Hight's house.

A yell issued from the jailhouse, then a shot.

'They're makin' a break!' screeched someone's voice, half drowned in the staccato roar of firing as Billy Hornby and Bob Davis fanned their .45s into the windows and doorway of the jailhouse. More yells followed.

A bullet whined past Sudden's head as he reached the corner of the stable and then he was around it, lungs tortured for breath, running as fast as he could drive his legs.

Again the staccato roar of shots boomed from the stable windows and he heard someone shout 'Get down, get down!' as the well-aimed barrage from his friends burned across the street. Now he was in the deep shade of the stable, slowing to a sliding walk. Dashing the perspiration from his eyes, he fell prone to the ground, moving on elbows and knees through the deep dust towards the picket fence which surrounded the back of Doc Hight's house. He wormed behind it, edging belly-flat across the sun-dried kitchen garden. His progress seemed maddeningly slow, but within a few more moments, he was within yards of the sloping edge of the arroyo which he had – was it only hours ago? – utilised to come up to the medico's house unobserved. His slitted eyes scanned the empty ground ahead of him, his ears were alert for the sound of running feet, but nothing moved.

Behind him gunfire boomed. He paused a second, listening. The Cottons were firing now.

'Hopin' to make the boys duck down, so they can send

110

someone out after me,' he muttered. 'Keep 'em pinned down, Billy!' The rolling boom of twin six-shooters joined in, and he smiled briefly to himself. Billy and Bob were still in business. He rolled over the edge of the arroyo. It was no more than four or five feet deep, and he had both guns out and ready as he came to a stop. Now he crouched down, moving slowly forward, using only his knees and elbows, utilizing every rock, every sparse shrub for cover. The ground was broken, and sharp stones tore at his unprotected hands and arms. Ignoring the pain, his face as impassive as that of a hunting Comanche, he edged northward up the arroyo. Presently it bore sharply to the left. He eased up against the left-hand wall.

'About level with the stable now,' he breathed. 'If I'm right, them jaspers oughta be just around this corner.'

As if in reply to his thought, he heard a cough. Metal chinked thinly; there was a shuffling sound. Someone moving his position, the puncher told himself.

'What the hell's goin' on out there?' he heard a voice mutter, very close. 'I heard yellin'.'

'Never mind what yu heard,' snapped another voice. 'Jest keep that door covered like yu was told.'

Green's brow furrowed. Two men had spoken. Was there a third? There was no way to tell, and only one way to find out. He straightened and stepped out into the open.

'Drop yore guns!' he snapped.

The scene before him erupted into action. The three men who had been lying on the sloping face of the arroyo under the shade of a thinly-leafed shrub tree whirled about, trying desperately to bring their Winchesters to bear upon this unexpected intruder. But Sudden had foreseen the reflex action and his guns were already blazing. The first shot whipped a big, bearded man backwards, erasing forever his astonished look. The second knocked down his companion, a runty individual wearing a blue shirt, hurling him flat and hard against the further wall of the arroyo, where he slid down in a slither of stones.

The third man was Jackson, the erstwhile gaoler whom Sudden had last seen bound and gagged in the jailhouse.

Jackson was moving fast even as Sudden's first shots were smashing his comrades to the ground, and he levered off a shot which tugged gently at the sleeve of the puncher's shirt. Sudden, too, was moving, dropping to one knee to confuse Jackson's aim, firing as he did so. His bullet hit the man high in the chest, tearing him off his feet. Jackson fell, rolling, a groaned curse of pain forcing its way from his lips, but clawing for the gun at his side.

'Don't do it, Jackson!' yelled Sudden. His guns were levelled and for a fraction of a second, Jackson hesitated, his darting eyes filled with pain. Then, in one movement, he grabbed for the revolver and tried to roll heavily to one side. The move might have confused another man, but Sudden's .45 blasted again, and Jackson fell back; a leg twitched, and he was dead.

Within a few more minutes, Sudden had gathered together the cartridge belts of the dead men. His lips turned to disappointment when he saw how sparsely filled were the belt loops.

'Still, any's better'n none,' he consoled himself, and then scrambled up the shelving slope of the arroyo wall, and moved rapidly across the open ground towards the stable. Doc Hight, he saw, had already moved out, and was poised now at the corner of the stable, peering around it, ready to break across the open space. Sudden waved the doctor on as he moved towards the door and heard the two men inside lay down their covering fire across the street.

Hight moved away towards his house and Sudden watched in a fever of suspense as the doctor negotiated the open space between the stable and his own house. No shots sought him, however, and in a few moments he was within a few paces of his own back porch. Sudden heaved a sigh of relief: it looked as if Hight had made it. The medico lifted a hand. Then he turned towards the door of his house.

Sudden turned now, slamming shut the rear door and dropping the heavy bar once more into place. Billy Hornby turned to face him from his post at the window, his face grimy with powder stains. His teeth gleamed whitely.

'Enjoy yore trip?' he asked whimsically. 'Yu wasn't gone long.'

112

'Seemed long enough to me,' retorted Sudden. 'I suppose it would depend on where yu was sittin'.'

Davis watched them. Their casual acceptance of danger, their ability to joke about it, was incomprehensible.

'How many o' them was out there, Jim?' he asked.

'Three,' was the grim rejoinder. 'They won't draw their pay.'

A chill ran through Davis's veins. Although he knew that the point of no return was long past, and that now it was kill or be killed, Sudden's icy words brought home the reality as so far nothing else had done. His mind lingered for a moment upon the possibilities of what Sim Cotton might do to them should Doc Hight not bring back the extra ammunition they needed. He swallowed deeply. Seeing this, Sudden sought to divert Davis' thoughts. Fear was beginning to touch the man like some corrosive acid. Maybe conversation would delay it a little.

'What's happenin' out there in the street, Bob?' he asked.

'Nothin',' mumbled Davis. 'They're keepin' their heads down.'

'Right smart o' them,' growled Billy. 'Although they was quite keen to come out an' see what yu was up to, Jim.' He smiled again. 'We kinda convinced 'em it warn't healthy.'

Sudden grinned. 'I'm bettin' yu did, too. Thanks just the same.'

'No thanks needed,' said Billy jauntily. 'It was purely a pleasure.'

Davis shifted uncomfortably at his post and Sudden regarded the storekeeper with narrowed eyes. Davis was living on his nerves, the puncher surmised. A faint twitch at the corner of one eye revealed the pressure the man was under, and his words confirmed it.

'What's keepin' Hight?' he muttered. 'He' been gone long enough, ain't he?'

'Give him a chance,' Sudden told the storeman. 'He ain't loiterin' none, yu can bet.'

Davis nodded, but his face was still set. He passed a hand over his eyes.

'My Gawd, I'm tired,' he confessed. 'Shore seems like a hell of a long day.'

His companions nodded quietly in agreement. Sudden did not feel it wise to voice his private thoughts – that somehow he was sure the worst was yet to come. Such a remark would scarcely help Davis, to whom such incessant tension was totally alien.

His thoughts turned to the medico. Hight, too, was unused to gun war, and so was the boy. Both of them had shown remarkable fortitude, but that would be of little help if they did not soon replenish their waning stocks of ammunition. He had divided the bullets retrieved from the men in the arroyo into three piles, each containing fourteen bullets.

'I'm hopin' Sim Cotton don't plan on rushin' us,' he thought. 'Otherwise it's goin' to be a short war.'

He wondered for the tenth time how the doctor was faring.

CHAPTER SEVENTEEN

Buck Cotton was not dead.

When Billy Hornby's panic-stricken horse had stampeded off the street, dragging him behind it screaming, and helpless as a sack of flour, the half-Indian boy who worked as a horse-wrangler for Sim Cotton had been with the Cottonwood remuda. All of Cotton's men had tethered their horses behind the sheriff's shack, the boy Pasquale posted with them to prevent their being startled into stampeding away by the shooting.

As the horse hurtled around the house, Pasquale had acted almost without conscious volition, for his life's training had been in controlling half-wild animals. He had leaped forward, throwing his wiry arms like steel bands around the animal's neck, clamping fingers like iron into the flaring nostrils, plunging his high heels deep into the yielding, slowing dirt, dragging the horse to a sunfishing, snorting stop almost by brute force. Eager hands had held the plunging, trembling animal; a razor-edged knife had parted the lariat in one sweeping slice. And they had pulled Buck Cotton to safety away from the murderous hoofs, carried him into the sheriff's rude abode, and laid him upon the lumpy bed. There Buck Cotton lay now. His face was raw and pulped, a mass of torn flesh; the skin of his arms and hands had been stripped off, ripped away by the scouring dust and stones of the street. His clothes were in tatters, ragged and blood spattered, and his hair was matted with dirt and gore. Buck Cotton tossed feebly on the bed, moaning, cursing with pain. Sim Cotton stood regarding him dispassionately.

115

'Pity yu wasn't killed,' he told the half-conscious figure on the bed. 'Yu shore ain't no help to us this way.'

Art Cotton moved across the room, his expressionless eyes fixing those of his older brother.

'Take it easy, Sim,' he said. 'It warn't his fault.'

'Not his fault?' snarled Sim Cotton. 'Yu think I give a damn whether it was his fault or not? All I know is that this whole stinkin' town seen my kid brother paraded in here like a 'pache squaw, with a rope round his neck. Damn him! An' damn that misfit cowboy who started all this!' He stalked across the room, glaring out of the window at the blank wall of the stable across the street.

'He was on'y doin' what yu told him to do,' remonstrated Art Cotton. 'Tryin' to get the kid's sister . . .'

'An' he made a mess of it, o' course,' jeered Sim. 'That two-bit nester kid outsmarted him.'

'He outsmarted all of us, Sim,' the other pointed out. 'It was as if they knowed all along what we'd do.'

'Bah, pure luck!' flung Sim Cotton. 'They're fools for luck, but I ain't through yet by a long chalk. Not by a long chalk,' he muttered, as if confirming his own thoughts. He sat down heavily in a wicker chair, staring moodily at his own boots.

Art Cotton touched his younger brother's shoulder.

'Yu all right, Bucky?' he asked, helplessly.

A groan was his only reply. Art looked at the half-Indian boy, who had been trying to clean Bucky's bloody face. Pasquale regarded him impassively.

'Bucky hurt bad,' he offered.

'I know it, damn yu!' ground out Art.

'Need doctor,' added Pasquale imperturbably.

Sim Cotton jumped to his feet, his brows lowered, his gaze intense, almost insane. He had no feeling for his young brother's hurt, and was only conscious of the deep wound to his own pride witnessed by the town he had thought of as his own personal property.

'Doctor him, then!' he thundered. 'Quit yammerin' about it.' Pasquale shook his head, his expression wooden.

'I not doctor,' he said.

116

'Pasquale's right, Sim,' Art Cotton added. 'He needs a real medico.'

Sim Cotton took a deep, deep breath, then released it as a growl of exasperation.

'Art, yu goin' soft in yore old age?' he grated. 'So the kid needs a medico. Yu can't be so stupid that yu don't know there's only one medico in this fleabag of a town, an' yu been tradin' slugs with him for nigh on an hour. Yu fixin' to amble over to that stable an' ask him real nicely to come out an' tend to Bucky?' He laughed; an ugly, mirthless sound. 'He'd spit in yore face, an' so would I in his place.' He went on, larding his voice with heavy, cutting scorn. 'But don't let me stop yu. Go on over an' try it. Yu'll get a slug in yore gizzard, but it's yore gizzard. Go ahead – fly at it. There's the door – go fetch the doc.'

He made an expansive bow, and gestured towards the door. Art Cotton looked at him, flat, expressionless, for a long moment.

'Don't yu care none about Bucky?' he asked eventually.

'Not much,' was the callous reply. 'Not any more. He got hisself into this. Come to think of it, he got all of us into it.'

Pasquale stood up. A man better schooled in observing men than Sim Cotton might have seen the disgust behind the boy's impassive expression, but not the owner of the Cottonwood, consumed as he was with hatred.

'Could get into doctor house,' he offered. 'Get to river. Arroyo on other side of bridge lead to doctor house. Mebbe get med'cine.'

Art Cotton stood up as the Indian boy delivered himself of this, for him, unheard-of colloquy.

'Pasquale's right, Sim,' he said. 'A man could edge down to the river bottom, then work up the arroyo. Jackson an' the others'd be coverin' the stable. It could work.'

His brother nodded, his mind occupied with other thoughts. 'Go ahead if yu want to,' he said unfeelingly. 'I don't reckon it matters much whether yo're here or not. Yu ain't been worth a dime since that drifter whipped yu.'

His voice had suddenly turned cutting and cold, and he

turned to face his brother once more.

'I allus figgered that when the chips was down I'd be left to do the real fightin' on my own,' he went on. 'Bucky never was worth a damn, an' yu' – yu was only muscle at the best o' times. When there's brain work to be done, the Cotton family ain't up to much. Go on,' he sneered. 'Get some ointment for yore ickle brother. Damme if I don't put yu in skirts when yu come back.' His voice rose to a thunder. 'Get out, get out o' here! Damned nester kid's got more guts than all o' yu put together!'

Without a word, Art Cotton got up and went out of the back door. His mind was black with hatred of his older brother. For all these years he had mindlessly obeyed Sim's commands, carried out without question the orders to oppress, to beat, to harass, and even to murder, never expecting to hear praise, doing it simply because Sim was Sim, and you no more questioned Sim Cotton's commands than anyone had ever questioned while he was alive the orders of Zeke, their father. And now this casual, slow-talking drifter had blown Sim Cotton's world apart and Sim himself was teetering on the edge of madness. Art considered for a moment. Supposing ... the thought was frightening, then the whiplash words his brother had just spoken stiffened his resolve. He pursued the thought which had insinuated itself into his head. Just suppose ... suppose that Sim did go over the edge? Suppose that something happened to him – something else? Something fatal, or even for that matter something crippling. Who then would lead the Cottonwood men? Who would reap the rich, fat rewards for which Sim Cotton had planned all these years? A wolfish grin turned Art Cotton's thin lips downwards. Yes, he thought, who? Would Bucky back Sim, if he knew how Sim had dismissed him, consigned him to death without a thought? No, Bucky would not. Would any of the Cottonwood men care who led them? Those who were left would follow the strong man, the man who could pay their gunfighter's wage. Yes. And yes again. If this rebellion of the town was crushed, then he, Art Cotton, would assume control. Providing something happened to Sim. It might happen anyway. Sim looked ragged

118

at the edges now. It wouldn't take much more.

And if he survived?

'He won't,' grated Art Cotton, unaware that he had spoken aloud as he stood in the shadow of the house, his brow lowered in thought.

'He won't what, Art?' asked one of the riders, a thickset, heavy-moustached fellow called Whitey. Art recovered himself rapidly.

'Bucky,' he told the rider. 'He won't live. Unless we get some stuff for his wounds. Yu better back me, Whitey. Yu, too, Nick,' he said to a second rider who was keeping a watchful eye on the stable from his post at the corner of the house.

'What's up, Art?' asked the latter.

'Bucky,' explained Art Cotton. 'He's bad hurt. I aim to slide over an' get some medicine an' stuff from Hight's place. Yu boy're comin' with me. I'll be needin' someone to cover me. Hight's in the stable with the puncher an' the kid, so I ain't expectin no trouble at the house but – I might need some cover fire if they spot me. I ain't plannin' on gettin' boxed in there.'

Whitey and Nick nodded. Theirs was not to question the wisdom of Art Cotton's plan – they were paid to do his bidding and no questions asked. Exposing themselves to danger was part of that. They fell in alongside him, and together the three of them moved cautiously back behind the house, using the jail building as further cover as they edged down towards the river. They reached the brush-speckled, shelving bank without incident and Art Cotton led the way down, sliding a little on the clay-slick earth, half crouching, sloshing ahead of his two riders towards the bridge carrying the road out of town which lay on their left.

'Jackson an' Platt is up there behind the stable with Caldecott,' Art told them. 'But they won't see us from where they're cached.'

'Yu better be right,' mumbled Whitey grimly. 'I ain't hankerin' after bein' cut down by one o' my own sidekicks, an' that's whatever.'

Art Cotton half turned, his face contemptuous.

'Cold feet, Whitey?' he jibed.

'It ain't cold feet to be careful about gettin' a slug in yore belly,' retorted Whitey unabashed.

'Hell,' scoffed Nick, whistling past the graveyard, 'They got more sense'n that, shorely?'

'I allus reckoned Bill Hickok had more sense than enough,' Whitey recalled, 'but he still managed to shoot down his own deppity in Abilene one time.'

'Keep quiet!' hissed Art Cotton. 'Yu fools jabber worse'n two kids on a picnic!'

The two riders lapsed into silence as Art sloshed out of the river bed and, bending low, scurried up the bank and dived face downward to the ground in the shallow arroyo. He wormed forward, Whitey and Nick close behind him. Presently they were opposite the rear of Hight's house. The open space between their shelter and the back door of the house gaped before them. Art Cotton surveyed it warily.

'Can't see the boys none,' he muttered. 'An' them jaspers in the stable ain't advertisin' which window they're at, neither.' He lay on the sloping arroyo wall, whipping his nerve.

'Hell,' he decide aloud. 'They can't see us none.' He got to his knees, crouching low. 'Come on!'

He clambered up over the arroyo edge, scuttling forward over the dusty open ground towards Hight's house. The two Cottonwood riders, after a moment's hesitation, darted after him. They reached the house in a bunch, panting, sweat drenching them. No shots broke the silence.

'Told yu so,' gasped Art Cotton. 'Come on.'

Within another minute they were in the house. It was hot and close inside, for the blinds had not been drawn and the sun's fierce rays had inexorably raised the temperature in the building.

'Keep yore eyes skinned,' Art Cotton ordered his men. 'Yu, Whitey, take the front window. Nick, yu watch the back. No shootin' unless yu got to. Yu hear me? I'm goin' to see if I can find anythin' that'll help Bucky.'

He barged into the small room which Hight used as a study and for seeing his patients. In it were only a desk, a small leather-covered table, a swivel chair and two wooden upright chairs by the window. Against the wall stood a glass-fronted cupboard. In it were some simple surgical instruments, an array of bottles and boxes. Art Cotton slid over to it, careful to avoid showing himself at the uncovered window.

'Ought to be somethin' in here,' he muttered. A swift blow from his pistol barrel shattered the pane of glass fronting the cupboard, obviating the necessity of finding a key for the small padlock on the door hasp. A vicious curse escaped Cotton's lips. His gaze revealed that the labels were all incomprehensibly inscribed in some unreadable scrawled language. Had he been able to, Art Cotton might have recognised it as Latin, but as it was, his reaction was simply to clumsily grab whichever of them looked as if might contain what he needed. He began to thrust them into the deep pockets of his chaps.

'I'll sort 'em out later,' he muttered. 'Damn that medico for a quack, labellin' his junk thataway. . . .' He swept aside the gleaming instruments, grinding their delicate forms to a twisted mass of metal beneath his angry heel. Wheeling around, he kicked over the leather-covered table, reducing it to kindling against the remains of the cupboard.

He was looking wildly about for something else to break when without warning a blasting of shots from somewhere in the back of the house brought his head up like that of a hunted animal.

'What the h—' he snarled as he whirled about, moving in haste into the larger area of the living room. He found Nick and Whitey peering anxiously through the back windows, their bodies flattened against the wall of the house.

'What in the name o' Satan's goin' on?' he barked. 'I told yu—'

'It warn't us, Art,' interposed Nick. 'Sounded like it come from the arroyo.'

'Mebbe they tried to make a break for it, an' the boys made 'em think again,' hazarded Whitey. 'It's shore stopped now.'

They listened in silence for another few moments, then Art Cotton nodded.

'Yo're probably right at that,' he conceded. 'Anyway, I got

what I came for. It's time to get out o' here.'

He moved over to the door, and was about to turn the handle when a stifled exclamation escaped the lips of Whitey, who was still peering out of the window.

'Hold it, Art!' snapped the man. 'Somethin's up!'

Cotton leaped over to the window, his eyes slitted, his figure tense.

'What was it?' he rapped out.

'I seen that Green feller harin' across towards the stable from the arroyo – *hell*!'

Art Cotton followed Whitey's pointing finger, and a thin whistle escaped through his teeth. Slowly, a grin of unholy glee appeared on his face. He laughed like a jackal.

'It's the medico!' he gasped unbelievingly. 'Green musta made some kind o' diversion to give him time to break out.' He pulled back from the window, gesturing the two riders to do likewise.

'The medico,' he breathed, and the cold flat light was back in his eyes for the first time since he had confronted Sudden in the street of Cottontown. 'An' he's walkin' right into our hands!'

CHAPTER EIGHTEEN

'Howdy, Doc!'

Art Cotton's voice was wicked and level and low and Hight recoiled, his hand moving back from the door handle as if it had suddenly turned into a rattlesnake. He half turned as though to break and run for it, his mouth opening to yell a warning.

'*Don't yu!*'

Art Cotton's voice had hardly changed, but Hight sensed the evil desire in it now, the just-suppressed urge to kill, as distinct as the rock-steady revolver in the Cottonwood man's hairy paw. It's bore yawned at Hight; and he could see the whiteness of Cotton's trigger-finger knuckle. One fraction of an ounce of pressure and he was a dead man. His mind raced. How had they known? How had they foreseen what Sudden would do? How had they got here? Did they know how short of ammunition the beleaguered men were? He let his muscles go slack, allowing a puzzled frown to settle on his face.

'What are you doing here?' was all he said.

'Oh, we just dropped in,' grinned Cotton evilly. 'Seemed like a nice day for visitin'.' He motioned with the gun. 'Get in here afore yore pards start wonderin' why yore loiterin' on yore own doorstep.'

Hight came into the house, his hands carefully held level with his shoulders. Art Cotton turned to Whitey.

'Any movement out there?'

The man at the window shook his head.

'Nary a sign, Art.'

Cotton turned to face Hight, planting his feet apart and thrusting his face forward until it was within inches of that of the medical man.

'Well, now, Doc,' he leered. 'We seen yore sidekick Green goin' back into the stable, which means he was creatin' some kind o' diversion. Now why would he want yu to sneak out, stead o' hisself?'

Hight made no reply.

'I'm guessin' Green managed to surprise my men,' whispered Cotton, his voice held deadly low. 'Which adds to the score he's goin' to pay. But it don't explain why yu come out alone, Doc. Yu want to tell me?'

Hight managed to inject some surprise into his voice, praying that Art Cotton would not detect any quaver in it.

'They said they were coming out behind me, as soon as I was clear . . .' he bluffed.

Art Cotton shook his head, his expression coldly mocking.

'No, that won't do, Doc. Yu can do better than that. I'll give yu one more chance. Why did they send yu out, an' why did they send yu here?'

Hight desperately tried another tack.

'The boy,' he gasped. 'He's wounded. I needed things . . . to dress his wound.'

'The kid was at the window throwin' lead not half an hour ago,' interposed Whitey's flat voice. 'I seen him.'

'So. . . .' Art Cotton whispered. 'Lyin' to me again, Doc?'

'No . . . I . . .'

'Liar!'

Cotton's screamed accusation was accompanied by a wicked backhanded blow to Hight's face. It sent the doctor reeling backwards, slamming against the wall, blood welling from a gash on his cheekbone caused by the heavy signet ring on Art Cotton's finger.

'No. . . .' Hight managed, holding up a shaking hand. 'I'm telling you the truth!'

Art Cotton stepped forward after him, his hands at his sides, a snarl disfiguring his face.

'No – yu – ain't!'

Each word was punctuated by another slashing blow. The third dropped Hight to his knees, fighting for consciousness. He fought against the panic in his mind: this man was insane, he would beat him to death. Art Cotton towered over him, his long fingers working, an empty light in his catlike eyes.

'They . . . they told me . . . to make a run for it,' Hight mumbled.

'Liar again!' Cotton's voice crackled like a whip. 'Yu wasn't tryin' to get away – yu headed for yore own house!' The fist drew back again. 'Why, damn yu?'

Hight cringed backwards. 'No – I'm tellin' yu the truth . . .'

Cotton reached down angrily, grabbing Hight's blood-spattered shirt in his meaty fists, hoisting the doctor to his feet. He thrust his face forward until the cold empty eyes were no more than a few inches away from Hight's own.

'Yu better tell me Doc,' he hissed, 'or yu won't get off with just a broken leg next time.'

Hight shook his head, dazed.

'You . . . you?' he managed. 'I always thought. . . .'

'It was Dave Rodgers? Shore, he was there, Doc. But *he* never broke yore leg.' A sneering smile was on the Cottonwood man's lips.

A reckless, seething, quite foreign rage seized Hight. This, then, was the man who had crippled him! The anger ousted all the physical fear from his mind, leaving only a cold and empty anger. Without thinking, he spat in Art Cotton's face. It was probably the bravest thing he had ever done, and he regretted its futility.

Art Cotton's face contorted with rage and his fist smashed forward. Hight felt a blow between his eyes, the searing snapping pain as his nose was broken, and the warm gush of bright blood. The room went black and spun away and when he could see again he was lying face down on the floor, not thinking, his brain disconnected by shock. Waves of pain blurred his vision, but he could vaguely see, far above him, the blurred form of Art Cotton. The man's leg moved, and Hight saw light flicker on the shining leather of a boot. The boot thudded into his ribcage, and an agonising pain spread throughout his chest and back. He felt as if something was broken inside of him, and he let the blackness come down again, welcoming it, escaping into it. It seemed to last a long time. He felt himself being hauled upright and tried to open his eyes but something seemed to be stopping him from doing so. He did not know that both his eyes were rapidly closing, his broken brows horribly swollen, or that a huge contusion of oozing blood marked the point where Art Cotton's massively punishing blow had broken his nose. His hands moved feebly, and somewhere in the back of his mind he felt a terrible fear that Cotton had blinded him, but then his vision cleared slightly. He was pinned against the wall by Cotton's grasp on his coat lapels. He tried to put his weight on his legs, but they were rubbery and weak. Cotton's voice came to him across years of time. It said something. A question. He shook his battered head.

'Go . . . to . . . hell.'

He heard a smashing sound inside his own head and then the blackness came. He slid into it gratefully.

Cotton turned away from the slumped body of the doctor, his face an insane mask of hatred.

'Nick!' he managed hoarsely. 'Get some water!'

The rider, who had watched aghast as his employer had battered the doctor, nodded hastily and edged past Hight's unconscious form, returning in a moment from the kitchen with a milk can full of water. This he handed to Art Cotton, who deliberately dashed it into Hight's swollen face.

The doctor groaned weakly, pawing at his face; he tried to sit up but could not. Once more Art Cotton pulled him upright, holding Hight on his feet by sheer brute strength.

'Still feelin' cocky Doc?' Cotton grated, 'or are yu ready to talk?'

He shook Hight the way a terrier shakes a rat, cruelly, viciously, furiously. Hight's head lolled. 'Talk, damn yu!' screeched the Cottonwood man. 'Talk! Talk! Talk!'

Hight's head lifted slowly. He peered at his tormentor through the slit of one eye.

'Yu'd better kill me, Art,' he mumbled through his torn lips. 'You'd better kill me, or as sure as God is my judge, I'll kill you. I don't know when, but I'll do it, I'll—' With a scream of uncontrolled, inarticulate rage, Art Cotton smashed the doctor backwards against the wall with a blow which carried every ounce of his weight. Hight was unconscious before his careening body bounced off the wall and slid to the floor. A thin pool of blood began to stain the carpet where he lay.

'My Gawd, Art!' breathed Whitey, 'yu've killed him shore.'

'Damn him for a pullin' crawling' swine, an' damn yu, too!' hissed Art Cotton, his chest heaving. 'Mind yore own damn' business! If he's dead—' he controlled himself with an effort as he said the words, 'it's good riddance.'

He stood swaying, rage gradually dying from his features, looking down at the prostrate form at his feet. As the disfiguring anger left his face, it was replaced by another expression, one of dawning realisation, then triumph, quickly replaced by cunning. He laughed, almost hysterically.

'I got it, by God!' he croaked. 'Why in hell didn't I think of it afore?'

Nick and Whitey exchanged glances. Had Art gone mad?

'What . . . What is it, Art? Whitey ventured.

Cotton regarded his men as if they were idiots.

'Yu can't see it?'

The two men shook their heads, frowning. Art's gloating, crooning voice, the spittle formed about his mouth, the mingled expression of triumph and cunning, all supported their fear that Cotton had gone insane, but when he spoke again it was in a normal tone, and the madness had left the cat eyes.

'So Sim thinks I'm all washed up, does he?' he muttered. 'I'll show him about that.' He began to pace across the room, back, forward, back, his step that of a caged tiger. 'He's goin' to be sorry he wrote me off,' he mumbled. 'Sorry. Very sorry. Yu'll see. It'll all be mine. I'll get them, an' it'll all be mine.' He looked up quickly. 'Yu boys with me?'

Whitey nodded hurriedly. 'Shore, Art, shore.' His tone was mollifying.

127

'Good,' Art nodded, pacing again. 'That's good. I'll need yu boys.' His mind was racing wildly, for in truth the violence of the past fifteen minutes had partially unhinged a mind which had never fully been sane. He issued a command. Whitey looked at him in amazement.

'What do yu mean, take his clothes off?' he managed.

'Yu stupid clod, do what I tell yu an' don't argue!' screeched Art. 'Strip his clothes off him.' He whirled on Nick, who cringed away. 'Yu, Nick!' He made an impatient gesture. 'Get yore clothes off.' Nick hesitated momentarily, and Art Cotton slapped his thigh impatiently, keening in rage. 'Do it, damn yu!' Nick shrugged, and began to unbutton his shirt as Whitey stripped off Hight's coat, boots, pants and shirt. Art Cotton watched the procedure, nodding throughout, muttering, 'Good, good.' The two riders, their tasks complete, looked at him for further instructions. He ground out an oath.

'Yu still can't see it, can yu?' he swore. 'O' course, I'm mebbe expectin' too much. All right, I'll spell it out. Nick – put on Hight's clothes. Yo're goin' to play decoy.'

Nick frowned yet again. 'Decoy?' Art Cotton's plan dawned on both of the gunmen in the same moment, and their laughter was a commingling of relief and admiration. The slow smile of evil spread on Whitey's dark-moustached face.

'O' course,' he breathed. 'They're expectin' him back?'

'O' course,' sneered Art Cotton. 'Took yu long enough to get it.' The wild light was still in his eyes but it was cold now and contained, under a form of control. He inspected Nick, dressed now in Hight's clothes, with malevolent satisfaction.

'Yu see it now?' he asked them. 'They sent him over here for somethin' – mebbe he was tellin' the truth an' it was medicine for the kid. Or mebbe they're low on water – or cartridges., even.' His smile was pure evil. 'That'd be even better,' he whispered, 'but it don't make no never-mind. Once I seen it – that they was expectin' him to come back – I seen how we could take them . . .' he snapped his fingers, 'like that!'

He began his pacing across the room again as Nick made the final adjustments to his disguise. His fingers clenched and unclenched, his thin lips worked as he prowled.

'So I'm not worth a dime, eh, Sim?' he spat. 'Well what does that make yore neck worth, damn yu?'

Then he stopped pacing and gave his men their instructions.

CHAPTER NINETEEN

Apart from a few sporadic, seeking shots from across the street, it had been quiet in the stable. Sudden had relieved Bob Davis at his post by the window, and the storekeeper was coaxing a reluctant fire underneath a coffee pot which he had found, half full, on a table near the rear of the building. The sharp, welcome tang of coffee filled the air.

'My belly's been thinkin' someone'd cut my throat,' Billy told nobody in particular, gazing hungrily towards where Davis hunkered over the tiny blaze. 'I ain't et since breakfast.'

'When this is all over I'll buy yu the biggest steak in the territory,' Sudden told him.

'Nix on that, Jim,' grinned the boy. 'I'm buyin'.' He heaved a huge sigh. 'I can see 'er now. A big, thick slab o' beef, with the juice runnin' all over the plate, an' mebbe three aigs on the top. A whole skillet full o' potatoes, brown an' crisp on the outside, soft as butter in the middle. Three pounds o' beans, mebbe—'

'Was yu brung up by 'paches, mebbe?' Sudden asked the boy, smiling. 'Yu shore know how to make a feller scream for mercy.' He watched idly as Bob Davis walked over to the window at the rear of the stable. 'Yu ain't the only one who ain't–'

'Here comes the Doc!' Davis's voice cut off Sudden's mild complaint, and the puncher moved backwards away from the window, careful not to expose himself, as Davis stepped away from his lookout, his hand reaching towards the door.

'Hell, he shore ain't hurryin' none,' complained the storekeeper. 'Come on, Doc, shift yoreself.'

A faint frown touched Sudden's forehead, and with a sharp admonition to Billy to keep the street covered, Sudden slipped quickly across the stable floor towards the window through which Davis had observed the doctor's approach.

'Anythin' moves, blast at it as fast as yu can pull the trigger, Billy!' he called over his shoulder to the boy, as Bob Davis slid the heavy bar away from the door. Sudden reached the window as Davis swung the door ajar. The storekeeper poked his head around it and leaned out, calling hoarsely 'Hurry up, Doc, for Gawd's sake!' Even as the words left his lips Sudden was yelling 'Slam that door!' and Davis turned his head sharply, startled. As he did so Hight's figure lurched forward into a flat run and Sudden saw the flickering movement of two more shapes below the level of the window still moving fast for the door. A blast of shots exploded in the doorway as he moved back and to the side to cover Davis and the storekeeper catapulted back inwards, twisting, falling across the threshold of the door, his feet kicking high.

With a shouted warning to Billy, Sudden's hands flashed to his guns as three men loomed dark and huge in the doorway, their guns blazing wildly into the semi-gloom, their seeking shots blasting across the position he had just vacated. In this fraction of a second, Sudden recognised the contorted face of Art Cotton. Then the intruders burst in to the stable, falling prone in scurrying, rolling movement, their action kicking up a thin, sun-speckled cloud of dust and chaff.

Now Sudden's guns were answering. The puncher had dived sideways towards the stalls on the left of the stable, moving fast and dropping on to his rounded shoulder, as lancing flames from deadly muzzles sought to level on his rolling shape.

Sudden felt something like a red hot iron being drawn across his ribs, all in this one long, endless second, the hammers of his own weapon falling with incredible speed, hearing the rolling blast of Billy Hornby's gun behind him. The man who had impersonated Doc Hight was doubled over just outside the doorway, his hands clutching his stomach, his head almost touching the floor. A second man, heavily-moustached, was careering sideways, torn off his feet by Billy's rapid roll of low-aimed shots. The stable was full of powder smoke and the whirring whine of whistling lead and the doorway was empty and there was the ugly sound of men dying.

And then there was a brief, empty silence and then as Sudden reached the end of his roll and gained his feet, there before him, mouth drawn back from his teeth in an animal snarl, was Art Cotton, lurching forward, the front of his shirt black with blood, his eyes empty, desperately striving to raise the gun in his hand while it grew heavier as the strength pumped out of his body.

'Damn yore eyes!' screamed Art Cotton, thumbing back the hammer of the gun and bringing it slowly up. Ere he could press the trigger, flame flashed from Sudden's hip and Cotton staggered, pitched sideways and slid to the floor, the weapon dropping from his twitching fingers. Sudden shoved his smoking .45 back into its holster and rose slowly, shaking his head.

'I had to do it,' he said, almost to himself. He looked at Billy across the stable floor. Smoke drifted lazily on the still air and there was the reek of cordite. They stood like this for perhaps three seconds, then Sudden snapped back into action.

'Back to yore window!' he shouted. 'Keep that street empty!' Billy leaped to his post, cursed, and laid four shots across the street. Several of the Cottonwood men who had been drawn from their lair by the sound of the gunfire inside the stable scattered, diving for cover as Billy's hastily thrown shots buzzed about them. In another moment, their return fire made the boy duck below the window frame as slugs whipped splinters from the woodwork and thudded into the walls. He turned to see Sudden bent over Bob Davis's still form. The puncher had slammed shut the rear door and the heavy bar was once more in place. Their eyes met. Sudden shook his head, straightening up slowly.

'He's dead, kid,' he said quietly.

Billy said nothing. There was nothing to say. His eyes moved to the coffee pot, bubbling now on the dying embers of the fire Davis had lit. He turned away from it quickly and looked at the blank, bullet-pocked wall in front of his eyes.

*

Sudden regarded the sprawled corpse of Art Cotton and of the moustached Cottonwood rider. He shook his head and walked to the window. Just outside the door lay the man who had been dressed in Hight's clothes, sprawled dead in a pool of blood.

'Looks like they got the Doc,' he told himself grimly. 'Only the devil's luck they didn't get us, too.'

It was a victory, but a bitter and unhappy one. Although three more of Sim Cotton's hired killers had come to the end of their nefarious careers, it was at a terrible cost. He shucked the empty cartridges from his guns, replacing them with bullets taken from the belts of the dead Art Cotton.

'Anythin' movin' on the street?' he finally said to his young companion.

'Not a thing, Jim.'

Sudden detected a note of weariness in the boy's voice. Billy stood slumped against the wall alongside the window. The fresh bright red of new blood stained his shirt.

'Yu opened that wound again,' Sudden admonished him.

'I was jumpin' around a mite,' admitted the kid. Then, 'Is Doc Hight . . . ?'

'That jasper outside is wearin' his clothes,' Sudden told him by way of reply. 'An' there's no movement over at the house.' A bitter round of curses flowed from the youngster's lips at these words. Sudden waited until Billy paused for breath, then told him, 'Cursin's like sittin' in a rockin' chair – it gives yu somethin' to do, but it don't get yu any place. At least we got some more ca'tridges.'

'It's a hell of a price to have to pay for 'em,' ground out the Lazy H man. 'I'd as lief done without.'

There was nothing to say to that, either. Sudden's bleak gaze moved to the window.

'Gettin' late,' he mused aloud. 'Be dark in a couple of hours.'

They sat in silence for several minutes, each busy with his own thoughts, both knowing that their thinking was along parallel lines. It was Billy who put them into words.

'Yu reckon they'll hit us again afore nightfall, Jim?'

Sudden shrugged.

'Hard to tell,' he admitted. 'They must know we're alone in here. Sim Cotton'll probably reckon he don't need to wait, but it depends on how many guns he can muster.'

'If they wait until it's dark, we ain't got much of a chance,' the boy murmured. 'Have we?'

'There's allus a chance, Billy,' the puncher told him gravely. 'Yu just have to wait until she pops her head up, then grab 'er.'

The faintest of whimsical smiles touched his lips as he spoke, but Billy's gloom was not to be so easily shifted.

'Hell, I'd feel better if we could do somethin',' he growled. 'I shore don't go much on this waitin' game.'

Guns ready at their sides, the two besieged men quickly scanned the empty street of Cottontown. At the far end, one or two lights were already glowing. It was very still.

'It's the on'y game we got,' was Sudden's quiet comment on the boy's complaint.

CHAPTER TWENTY

Alone in the cool gloom of the livery stable the two men waited. Billy sat with his back against the wall, the window to the right of his head. Without moving too much he could quickly scan the street to ensure that their enemies made no sneaking dash towards them. The town had stayed silent now for over an hour. No shots had been fired, no attack mounted on their redoubt. Sudden had taken advantage of the lull to staunch the flow of blood from the youngster's reopened wound by the simple expedient of stripping off the blood-stained bandanna which Doc Hight had put on, soaking it in water and twisting it dry. Billy had set his lips tight as Sudden bound up the ragged wound, and had even essayed a tight grin as the puncher had then stripped off his own shirt to dab water on the six inch bullet burn across his ribs.

'They won't get no closer to yu than that without interferin' with your breathin'. Need any help?'

Sudden grinned. 'If I feel faint I'll yell,' he said.

His medical chores completed, the puncher hunkered down on a bale of straw and began to roll a cigarette. Billy's cheerful words were good to hear. The kid had nerve enough for six men, but nerve alone was not going to get them out of this box. He pondered the reaction of the town to the wicked blows dealt to Cotton's prestige. Would anyone in this cowed little valley back them when the final attack started? That it would come, and soon, he did not doubt. There was no way of knowing when, or how. Cotton's force might be reduced but he still had enough guns to give two lone men, one of them able to use only his left hand properly, a pretty bad time of it when he struck.

As if divining Sudden's thoughts, Billy spoke aloud, his voice pensive and musing.

'I shore can't figure this burg,' he began. 'They musta seen all that's happened; they shore knowed we was buckin' Sim Cotton an' his toughs. Why ain't they pitched in to give us some support, Jim?'

Sudden shrugged. 'Hard to say. It'd go ag'in them if Sim Cotton come out on top – I'm guessin' he's a man with a long memory for things o' that nature.'

'I know that,' remonstrated Billy. 'But if we'd had six men in here who could use a gun, we coulda sent Sim Cotton an' his paid guns skedaddlin' for the hills an' set this town free o' him.'

'Mebbe that's the problem, Billy,' Sudden suggested quietly. 'Have yu given any thought to what happens to this town if Sim Cotton is broken?'

'Shore!' replied Billy stoutly. 'Every man jack in the place'll be his own man again, makin' his own livin', sellin' or buyin' as sees fit to anyone he wants to. That can't be bad, can it?'

'Depends,' his companion said. 'It's pretty easy to get into the habit o' lettin' someone else do yore thinkin' for yu. Once that happens, every day that passes makes it tougher to think for yoreself ag'in.'

'Shucks, Jim,' scoffed Billy. 'I ain't never felt thataway.'

'Yu ain't, mebbe,' Sudden reminded him, 'but mebbe a few o' the men in this town has. An' they ain't shore that gettin' rid o' one problem ain't just takin' in another. So they're sittin' tight, waitin'. If we come out o' this alive, they ain't no wuss off than afore. If we don't, then they ain't goin' to have Sim Cotton takin' after them for sidin' with us.'

Billy made a rueful face. 'I hadn't given it much thought along them lines,' he admitted. 'Could be yo're right. Yu've bin right about 'most everythin' else.' He bent a frowning gaze upon his friend. 'I dunno how yu do it. Yu ain't exactly elderly—'

'Well, thanks for that,' murmured Green.

'An' yet yo're wise to the way all kinds o' different folks see things. I ain't never seen a man so fast on the draw as yu are, but yu ain't that much older than me. How come, Jim?'

'Just luck, I guess,' came the reply, but Sudden's voice was far from light. Behind it Billy Hornby sensed a deep sadness and knew, without being sure why, that his words had burned deep into some corner of his companion's thoughts like salt rubbed into an open scratch.

'Hell, Jim, I shore didn't mean to pry—' he began, but Sudden cut him off with a gesture.

'Forget it,' he smiled. 'Yu wasn't to know. Some fellers has to learn the ropes in different schools to others, that's all.'

His mind went back into his own past. He saw himself again as he had once been, a thin, half-starved youngster roaming around the southwestern territories, more or less the property of the old Piute horse-trader who had raised him. He recalled the nomadic life, the slow turning of the seasons as they had moved from place to place, the eventual discovery that the Indian was not his father. And then the years with Bill Evesham. The kindly old rancher had taken a fancy to the nameless boy and 'bought' him from the old Piute, given him a name, a name which Sudden had discarded after the events which set him upon the trail of the two men he had vowed to his dying benefactor that he would find.

'I shore can't believe that all this has happened in on'y one day,' Billy began again tentatively. 'Seems like half a lifetime to me.'

At these hesitantly spoken words, Sudden shook off his thoughts of the past. 'I'm gettin' worse'n an old-timer,' he chided himself. 'Next thing yu know I'll be chatterin' about the good ol' days.' To the boy he said: 'Yo're right. She's been a mighty long day. Makes yu realise what them men in the Alamo went through when Santy Anna was tellin' his band to play the *deguello*.'

Billy knocked on the wooden wall and whistled. 'I hope she don't come out the same way,' he said, with a shiver.

'We got a fifty-fifty chance, anyways,' Sudden told him. 'Sim Cotton shore ain't got the weight he had when all this started. He's lost twelve men to our two.'

'That still leaves him mebbe three or four – not countin' hisself, an' I'm thinkin' yu'd have to hump yoreself, good as yu are, to beat Sim Cotton to the draw, Jim.'

Sudden looked up. 'He's fast, is he?'

'Like a rattler,' conformed Billy. 'He don't make no play about it, but some as have seen him in action reckon he could've given that Texas outlaw, Sudden, a run for his money.'

To this last remark the puncher made no reply, but the grim lines around his mouth deepened slightly. For the fiftieth time he wondered how, and when, the next move would come.

CHAPTER
TWENTY-ONE

It came about half an hour later.

Billy Hornby had eased himself carefully upwards to peer out from his vantage point at the window. As his eyes swept the empty street, he straightened quickly, gun cocked and ready. Noting the boy's reaction, Sudden was already rising swiftly and moving to his own window as the boy hissed excitedly, 'They're wavin' some kind o' flag out o' the jailhouse window.'

A glance confirmed to Sudden that a disembodied arm was indeed waving a dirty white rag tied to the end of a stick from the window across the street.

'Flag o' truce?' he muttered. 'What the devil–?'

Even as the words left his lips, the figure of a man stumbled out of the jailhouse door, faltering on the threshold as though unwilling to move further. Obviously someone had ordered him to go out into the silent, unwelcoming street, and was now insisting that the man proceed, however reluctantly. There was no mistaking the furtive stance, the unshaven visage, the stained and disreputable clothes.

'Kilpatrick!' breathed Billy. 'An' he shore ain't keen on his work.'

The decrepit old lawyer stepped tentatively towards the street, the sagging banner raised high in one hand.

'Parley!' he called hoarsely. 'Flag o' truce!'

'Looks like they wanta palaver,' suggested Billy. 'If this ol' goat can make hisself heard over the noise o' his knees knockin'.'

Sudden smiled. 'He looks a mite nervous,' he allowed, then raising his voice, called 'Come ahead, Judge – but come careful!'

'I ain't heeled!' screeched Kilpatrick, stopping in mid-stride in the centre of the dusty street. 'Don't shoot! I ain't heeled!'

'Yu better not be!' rapped Sudden. 'Come ahead an' say yore piece – but yore friends better not get any ideas: I'm tetchy jest now, an' if anyone makes me jump I'd just nacherly shoot yu right through the gullet.'

Kilpatrick's scrawny Adam's apple bobbed as he swallowed deeply. Billy Hornby squinted along the barrel of his gun laid already on the sill of the window. 'Shore is a real temptin' target,' he suggested.

'It is at that,' agreed Sudden, 'but yu couldn't pull the trigger any more'n I could.'

Billy sighed. 'Yo're right, o' course. I'm thinkin' I may regret it, just the same, afore tomorrow.'

Kilpatrick stood stock still in the street. Sweat trickled down his wrinkled jowls, glistening on his stubbled cheeks, soaking his shirt. It was clear to those watching that he was even having trouble holding the 'flag' steady.

'Nerves playin' yu up, Judge?' called Sudden, sardonically. 'Yu wasn't so shaky this mornin'.'

A fleeting expression of hatred twisted Kilpatrick's face, to be quickly concealed. But Sudden had seen the look and knew his jibing words had found their mark.

'I ain't shaky now, damn yu!' snapped Kilpatrick, a vestige of his old asperity returning to his voice. 'I'm offerin' yu a chance to ride out o' this town afore it's too late.'

'Yo're offerin' us a chance?' Sudden's voice was stiletto cold.

'Sim Cotton is willing to let you ride out of here and no hard feelings,' continued the old man.

'Mighty generous o' him,' retorted the puncher. 'What's the catch – there's gotta be one.'

'The terms are simple, Green. Turn the boy over to Sim and you ride out of here alive. Refuse, and you'll be carried out dead – both of you.'

The old voice was dry with venom. Kilpatrick squinted up at

the blank windows of the stable. 'You hear me, Green?'

'I hear yu,' came Sudden's flat reply. 'Now yu hear me, yu worthless hide, an' tell yore boss I'd sooner make a deal with Satan!'

Kilpatrick made one more attempt, his voice quavering.

'Yo're making a mistake, Green!'

Sudden's reply was not in words. Without seeming to aim, he planted a shot within an inch of Kilpatrick's right toe, the bullet chunking a gout of dust upwards. The old man leaped as though stung, his eyes bugging, a shrill screech issuing from his throat as he broke in voiceless terror, dropping the grubby flag of truce and scuttling back towards the jailhouse like a frightened rabbit. A ragged rattle of covering fire spattered into the walls of the stable as the two men ducked down.

Sudden grinned across at Billy, who grinned back. Then Billy's face turned serious.

'Jim, I'm thankin' yu again,' he essayed. 'Yu coulda rid out o' here—'

'Shucks, I wouldn't get twenty yards afore I got a slug in the back, an' yu know it,' Sudden said, 'so don't bother thankin' me none. I'm allus inclined to play things safe.'

'Shore,' Billy said, mock scorn in his voice. 'Yu play things safe. An' I'm Ulysses S. Grant.'

The puncher's smile widened. 'Thought yu looked familiar,' he said. 'Must be the beard.' Then before the boy could suitably reply he went on, 'Sim Cotton must be gettin' worried to try somethin' like that. What yu reckon he's up to?'

'Search me,' said Billy, 'but whatever it is, it ain't no good.' It was not to be many minutes before the two men were to discover the truth of this statement.

While Kilpatrick had distracted the attention of the two men in the livery stable, Sim Cotton's men had been busy. Two of them had sneaked up to the northern end of the town, using the houses as cover. One of them was the man called Ricky, a dirty bandanna tied around the lacerated scalp which had been the result of his earlier collision with the puncher. The other Cottonwood man, a burly fellow named Rolfe, lumbered along behind. They entered the vacant general

141

store, where Rolfe appropriated two large metal drums of kerosene. Then they scuttled across the empty street, out of sight of the two men in the stable, and worked their way down behind the bank, then the saloon, until they were close to the blind northern wall of the stable. They could see Kilpatrick in the street, and hear his exchange with the puncher.

Rolfe, the kerosene drums swinging at his side, looked questioningly at Ricky, who was piling refuse, dried leaves, bits of brushwood and any other rubbish which he could lay his hands upon, against the wall of the stable. When Ricky at last nodded, Rolfe swung the drums to the ground. Tearing the cap off one, he sloshed its contents heedlessly upon the pile of refuse. Ricky, following suit, splashed the contents of the second drum up against the walls, soaking the dusty timber and the ground around the bonfire. The canisters, now half empty, he laid upon the top of the pile, and then stood back, hands on hips, surveying the results of their efforts.

'Yu think it'll work?' whispered Rolfe hoarsely.

'It better,' his companion told him grimly, 'or Sim Cotton's finished, an' so are we.'

Rolfe nodded. Sim Cotton's plan had been murderously simple: to distract the men in the stable with a phoney parley while giving his men the opportunity to prepare this last-ditch attempt at forcing the besieged men into the open.

Ricky raised a hand as a signal, and then with a gesture to Rolfe to move out, struck a match and tossed it on to the kerosene-drenched pile. The kerosene ignited with a slight '*whoomp*!' and then the seeking flames bit deeply into the pile of rubbish and brushwood. Within a few seconds, long hungry tongues of questing flame were reaching up the side of the livery stable, blistering the ancient paintwork, feasting joyously upon the bleached wood of the building, as Sudden's contemptuous shot put Martin Kilpatrick to flight, and the two Cottonwood men faded back and headed by their circuitous route towards the jailhouse.

Sim Cotton, from his vantage point in the jailhouse, had watched the developments in the street with a cold and pitiless

142

smile. Kilpatrick's discomfiture – he did not deign to turn as the old man tumbled in from the street, fighting for breath and rigid with fear – was a tiny price to pay for the chance to lay these two rebels by the heels. Sim Cotton's mind had callously totalled the odds and found them wanting. Somehow, incredibly, this sardonic drifter and a dirt-poor youth had broken his hold on this valley, had cut his crew down until now there was only himself and two riders. His lip curled: he knew exactly how long he would have the loyalty of the remaining two if this last, desperate gamble failed.

'Dawgs,' he muttered to himself. 'Yeller dawgs. They figger if I win they'll get a bigger cut, an' if I lose they can crawfish out.' His black brain planned, twisted, discarded, appraised. The cowboy, Green, had he sent for the US Marshal? Was he bluffing or not? Sim Cotton shook his head. He could not take that chance. If a US Marshal was on his way, then Green and the boy must be dead before he arrived.

He glanced contemptuously at the huddled figure of Martin Kilpatrick, wheezing still in the darkened corner of the room.

'Ol' fool,' he thought, callously. 'Pity the slug didn't put him out o' his misery.' At this moment the rear door opened, and Ricky and Rolfe came in. Cotton lowered his quickly-cocked gun.

'How's she goin'?' Ricky said, easing over to the window. A coarse laugh escaped his lips as he surveyed the result of his handiwork. 'Pretty good,' he continued. 'Like a house on fire, yu might say.' Sim Cotton nodded but did not speak. He moved again to the window and peered out, his eyes reflecting the mad, dancing flames roaring now, crackling as they greed-ily bit into the desiccated wood of the stable. A half-insane chuckle gurgled in Sim Cotton's throat, freezing the blood in Ricky's veins, hardened though the man was. There was gloat-ing triumph in Sim Cotton's voice when he spoke, when he hissed out:

'Burn' damn yu, burn!' The insane laughter swelled. 'Fry the bastards!'

CHAPTER
TWENTY-TWO

'Fire!' yelled Billy Hornby. 'They've fired the stable.' He started to scramble down from his post by the window as the first heavy black plumes of smoke surged into the building and the dull crackle of the flames made itself heard.

'Stay where yu are!' rapped Sudden. 'Keep yore eyes on that street – I ain't pinin' to be rushed.'

He vaulted down to the floor, and as he did so, Billy's gun spoke twice.

'Right again, Jim,' he crowed. 'One o' them just stuck his head up for a looksee. I reckon he's plumb discouraged. How is it?'

Sudden had grabbed a bucket full of water which had been left in one of the stalls ready for the horses and sloshed it on to the rapidly charring timbers. Already the sound of the flames was a steady, solid roar, and the smoke grew ever thicker. The water seemed to check the flames for a brief moment, and then they surged forward again. Sudden sloshed the bucket into the half-full water barrel, and again, and again, hurling the water into the inferno which was now spreading through, and along, the entire wall of the stable. Each time he did so, the flames hissed, spluttered, retreated momentarily; by the time the bucket was refilled they had once more advanced. Sweat streamed off Sudden in the intense heat, and the flames licked out towards him hungrily, singeing his hair and eyebrows, scorching his shirt. Flickering sparks, tiny burning pieces of wood floated in the dusty, smoke-filled air as the

144

puncher laboured mightily to stem the flames. There was hardly any water left in the barrel now, although he had the feeling that he was containing the blaze. The flames had hardly advanced at all in the last few minutes and for a second, hope flared in the puncher's heart. Again he dashed the water into the flames. Was it just imagination? Or were the flames not spreading any further?

He threw the bucket into the barrel once more. It clunked leadenly against the bottom. A quick inspection revealed that there was only an inch or so of water left in the barrel and Sudden cursed silently at this reversal.

With a lithe spring he was behind Billy, who watched the street with eyes narrowed against the coiling smoke.

'Is it out?' asked the boy, without turning.

'Like hell,' gritted Sudden. 'We're out o' water.'

They looked at each other silently.

'No chance, then?' Billy said finally.

'We could try spittin' on it,' proposed the puncher. The boy tried a smile but it fell apart.

'Damn, damn, damn,' he muttered.

Now the smoke thickened, laying a level of darkness across the stable floor. The licking flames, quelled for a while in their inexorable march, now began to advance again, moving slowly at first and then more quickly as they caught dry wood once more. Unhampered now by the brief attempt to quell it, the fire crept steadily and surely up the wall, flickering along a beam in the roof and then another, and upwards into the slatted roof itself. The stink of scorching leather laced their nostrils as the fire, fanned by a faint breeze from the west, moved along the entire length of the northern wall and reached fiery fingers across the back wall. The roof beams were now firmly alight, charring rapidly. Great chunks of wood slithered downwards, flaming, sending up showers of angry sparks which smouldered and caught, caught and burned. The flames licked across the door at the rear, dancing lightly, delicately, almost beautiful. Sudden watched them for a moment, then shrugged. Within only a few more minutes the place would be an inferno. It was already unbearably hot; both men were bathed in sweat, their clothes sticking to them like second skins. Once the flames reached the stacked straw bales . . . Sudden's mind retreated from the pictures his imagination conjured up. There was only one way out left: the front way. The way covered by the waiting guns of Sim Cotton's killers. His mind worked furiously. To make a run for it would be suicidal. Surrender? Billy would surely never agree to such a humiliation. He would want to die fighting. Sudden planned, discarded, planned again, his brain plotting move and countermove furiously. Billy was down on the floor again, beating at the flickering sparks in the straw with his jacket. Beneath its sooty mask the boy's face was strained.

A stentorian yell from outside cut through the heavy crackle of the flames.

'Green! Can yu hear me?' It was Sim Cotton's bull voice, coming from the jailhouse.

'I hear yu!' shouted Sudden. Billy's soot-speckled face was stiff.

'Yu better surrender, Green! Yu ain't got a snowball's chance in hell. That place is goin' to fall in on yore head in about ten minnits. Yu ain't got a prayer – an' yu know it!'

The refusal sprang to Sudden's lips, but even as it did, he saw the bright fresh blood on Billy's shoulder. The frantic attempt to beat back the flames had again opened the wound, and he knew Billy was in no condition to make a run for it.

'Okay, Cotton!' he shouted. 'Yu win! We're comin' out!'

'No, Jim!' exploded Billy. 'They'll cut us down like dawgs!' Sudden made no reply, but gestured at the vivid tumbling flames which crawled ever nearer to them. Even as he did, a huge roof beam crashed to the floor, shattering into a thousand pieces of flying flame, starting flickering tongues of moving light dancing upon the tiers of straw bales all around them.

'Billy, we got about five minnits an' we're goin' to be dead, anyway,' Sudden gritted. He put a nervous tone in his words. His voice was thick with smoke but Billy could sense the bitterness underlying the words.

'Throw yore guns out ahead o' yu!' came the shouted

command from across the street. 'Then come out with yore han's up.'

'Do what he says, kid,' Sudden told the boy.

For a long moment, Billy Hornby hesitated. He looked at the gun in his hand. He looked, almost wistfully, across the street. Divining his thoughts, Sudden made his voice quaver.

'Throw yore gun out, Billy,' he ordered. He emphasised the words by cocking his own revolver and aiming it at the boy. Billy's eyes widened in astonishment, then disgust spread across his face.

'I never thought yu'd chicken out, Jim,' he rasped bitterly.

'I ain't about to be no dead hero,' grated Sudden. 'Throw it!' With a curse, Billy tossed his pistol out of the window into the dust. He scrambled down from the window and stood by the door as Sudden followed his example, sending the two .45s spinning far out to land half buried in the sandy street. The flames touched the two men as they edged past the smouldering bales of straw, their arms shielding their faces from the murderous heat. Coughing, retching, eyes streaming, Sudden threw back the heavy bar across the door and flung it wide. The new draught fanned the flames back for a moment, and then they surged forward as though in pursuit of the reeling, staggering figures who stumbled out into the street, their clothes dotted with tiny burns, gulping huge deep breaths of clean air into their labouring lungs.

As their vision cleared, they saw below them the hulking figure of Sim Cotton. Cradled in his meaty paws was a long rifle with an unusual, octagonal barrel and an old-fashioned hammer of the flintlock style. The receiver and stock were heavily chased with silver which caught the light of the roaring flames behind them.

'Hoist yore paws, yu vermin!' exulted Sim Cotton. 'I'm goin' to enjoy this!'

'Yu brung enough gun,' was Sudden's remark as he obeyed the Cottonwood owner's snarled order. 'That's a Sharp's buffler rifle, ain't it?'

Behind them there was a rumbling, roaring crash. The roof of the stable was sagging inwards. It would fall at any moment.

'Yu better let us step away a mite, less'n yore aimin' to fry, too,' Sudden told his captor.

For a moment the mad light in Cotton's eyes flared brighter, but then he nodded. He stepped back a few yards, beckoning the two silent men away from the blazing stable, the reaching flames lighting the twilit street with a red and gruesome cast.

Billy Hornby said nothing. He did not even look at his companion.

'Sharp's buffalo gun is right,' agreed Sim Cotton as he settled himself again in front of them. 'Throws a fifty-calibre slug. I seen one o' these knock a man down a half a mile off. Allus wondered what it'd do close to.'

For the first time since their surrender, Billy Hornby spoke. 'If yo're aimin' to kill us, get on with it, Cotton!' he rasped. 'Yo're gloatin' make me sick.'

Sim Cotton smiled, a satisfied, evil smile.

'Yu don't get off that light, boy,' he rumbled. 'I'm goin' to make an example o' yu in front o' this whole town. Take a look!' He gestured with his head and the prisoners turned to see the remaining two Cottonwood riders herding a crowd of hesitant, nervous townspeople forward, pushing them down the street like cattle ahead of their drawn guns.

'Cottontown is goin' to watch this,' gloated Sim Cotton, 'an' remember. They're goin' to watch yu die. An' they're goin' to see it every time they even dream about crossin' me again. This was my town afore yu come along. It's still my town! It's allus goin' to be my town! Mine, yu hear?' His voice had risen to a scream, and the milling crowd a yard or so away, held in check by the guns of Ricky and the burly Rolfe, held their breath in awe at his outburst. Sudden watched Sim Cotton from beneath veiled eyes. The man was quite insane now. There was a chance . . . a faint chance.

'Yu . . . yu wouldn't cut us down in cold blood, Mr Cotton?' he quavered, ignoring the look of utter contempt that Billy shot at him. 'Yu wouldn't just . . . we was only defendin' ourselves.' Sim Cotton threw back his head and laughed. He turned to the crowd, dominating the street like a mad animal, making those in front edge backwards.

148

'Yu see him crawlin'?' he roared. 'Yu see how tough he is, now he can't bushwhack my men an' hide in a barn? Yu see what happens when yu cross a man like Sim Cotton?' He made a gesture with his left hand. 'I snap yu – like this!' He snapped his fingers contemptuously and in that moment, the half unguarded moment while his left hand was in mid-air and the huge buffalo rifle wavered in his right, Sudden moved. His right arm shot sideways, jarring Billy Hornby off his feet, staggering aside with a look of astonishment crossing his face as his legs crossed and he fell, and saw, as he was falling, the man he had contemptuously called a coward dropping to his left, headlong and rolling, his hand moving towards the glinting metal of the gun which lay half buried in the dirt where he had thrown it from the blazing stable.

In the same half-second, with Sim Cotton's grandiose contempt freezing into astonishment as Ricky yelled 'Sim! Watch out!' and the townspeople scattered like a flock of quail out of the line of fire, men screeching in panic, bowling Rolfe off his feet, Sim Cotton wheeled, his left hand fanning back the eared hammer of the huge rifle, slanting the barrel down towards the snaking figure of Sudden now rising into a half-crouch with the Colt level and deadly in his hand. With a howl of rage and hatred Sim Cotton pulled the trigger of the long rifle, its dull boom smashing across the panicked shouts, drowning the lighter roar of the .45 in Sudden's hand. But Sim Cotton was dead on his feet when he pulled the trigger, a neat hole drilled between his rage-knitted brows by Sudden's unerring shot. Sim Cotton tottered, lurched, fell forward, folding like a broken grass stalk, slamming into the dusty street of the town that had once been his.

The big calibre bullet whanged off the wall of the saloon as Ricky laid his fire over the scrambling form of Billy Hornby, whipping the dust up as Sudden wheeled in one movement after firing the shot which had downed Sim Cotton, the gun in his hand roaring in a stuttering roll, slashing Ricky backwards with two bullets driven through his heart. In these blurring movements, Rolfe had regained his feet and was now rushing forward as Sudden whirled once more left, but Rolfe's gun was blazing, and Sudden was momentarily off guard. The breath-less watchers saw Sudden flinch slightly, staggering a pace backwards, his guns blazing even as he did, drilling his remain-ing two bullets into the running Cottonwood man, one in the heart, one in the head. Rolfe's screamed curse was cut in two and his gun fired by reflex action as he stopped in his running tracks, hurled back, down, by the smashing impact of the bullet. He tumbled slewed into a broken shape in the dust.

Sudden was on one knee, supporting himself with his left hand, his right pawing at his forehead. Rolfe's shot had caught him high on the scalp, just above the point of the hairline, half-stunning him, a thick trickle of blood nearly blinding the puncher. Unsure that he had stopped Rolfe, Sudden fired blindly into the red murk before his eyes, only to hear the hammer fall upon an empty shell. Not fully in command of his senses, he struggled to his feet, swaying, knuckling the blood from his eyes, his blood-slippery hand fumbling at his belt for shells to reload the gun, peering like an old man into the mist before him. He lurched forward a pace as Billy Hornby took a step from the porch of the saloon where he had rolled to escape the heedless bullets. Even as the boy moved, as the townspeople began to get to their feet, a remembered voice cut the hushed silence of the street.

'Green!'

Trying still to focus his blurred vision, shaking his head to get rid of its steady buzzing, not knowing that Rolfe's bullet had badly concussed him, Sudden half lifted the empty gun in his hand. The thin, terrible voice cut through the fog.

'Try it.'

He let his hand drop, shrugging. It had been a brave attempt, but they had beaten him. The voice ... which of them was it? Why did he know the voice? And then his eyesight cleared for a moment, enough for him to see the owner of the keening voice, the figure of the man he had thought dead – Buck Cotton!

The last of the tyrants stumbled down from the porch of the sheriff's house. A murmur of hushed awe escaped the clus-tered watchers for Buck Cotton was a sight to inspire horror, fear and pity. Dried and matted blood caked his hair, his face. His clothes were like those of some blood-spattered scarecrow, torn, trailing in strips and tatters, filthy. The skin of his exposed arms and legs and the back of his trembling hands was gone, leaving a raw exposed bloody mass, his twitching face was as red and angry as a peeled tomato, and his eyes were glaring with a wild and dislocated light. In his wavering grasp was a cocked rifle covering his quarry. He took three weaving steps forward. Nobody dared to move.

'Yu did this to me, yu swine,' whined Buck Cotton. 'Yu did this.' A sob of possessed rage swept through his frame. 'Yu killed Sim, too. Yu an' yore stinkin' nester friend ruined it all. But yo're goin' to pay, damn yu. I'm goin' to shoot yu to pieces, Green, yu hear? Shoot yu to pieces. Bit by bit, by bit by bit . . .' He cackled insanely, his laughter ending on a high choked note. 'Damn yu!'

His finger whitened on the trigger and Sudden, helpless and unarmed, steeled himself for the shock of the bullet. They said you hardly felt it, you only heard the shot. He winced as the explosion filled the air.

It did not come from the barrel of the rifle in Buck Cotton's hands. It came from a battered old Army Colt in the relentless grasp of Doc Hight. The medico, his face swollen almost out of recognition, stood like an angel of vengeance in the middle of the dusty street, the marks of the vicious beating he had received plain for all to see. His shot smashed into the stock of the rifle in Buck Cotton's hands, tearing it from his grasp, knocking him reeling back two paces. Hight's stentorian voice shattered the silence.

'What kind of town is this?' he cried to the watching crowd. 'Will you stand there and see the man who saved you be murdered? Will you never understand that you must fight to be free?' An animal sound escaped from Buck Cotton's mouth. He dived forward to get his hands on the rifle which had been torn from his grasp, a scream bubbling up insanely in his throat.

'I'll get yu, Green!' he screeched.

Sudden took a step forward but as he did so he heard a

strange and awful sound, the sound of a feral beast, the sound of men finally irrevocably committed to a path of violence. Sudden knew that sound. It was the sound of the awakened mob. Fighting desperately against the blackness which swam up into his head, he tried to shout, tried to hold back the violent tide of death, but rough, friendly hands thrust him aside, lifted him, and the sweet warm darkness began to fall and he cried out 'No!' to stop them. But even as he did so he heard a terrible, inhuman scream and knew that the men of the town had fallen like ravaging wolves upon the last of the Cottons.

CHAPTER
TWENTY-THREE

Far away, far away in the further reaches of his consciousness, Sudden could hear voices, and memory came slowly back into his brain like water spreading across sand. He remembered fire, and then the stable; he remembered the sight of a big man falling, folding forward like a broken blade of grass. He remembered . . . he remembered? He opened his eyes. The light was like a knife. Someone said. 'He's awake.'

A face looked down at him. It was a young face, a boy's face. Next to it was the face of a girl. They looked alike. Brother and sister? They faded out of sight. Another face. Bruised, yellow, purple, green, black. Swollen. Been in a fight.

Then the boy's face. He thought that the boy was crying.

'Don't cry,' he said, and then he fell asleep just like that, blackness slipping over him like a soft, comforting blanket. He slept for another three days without once opening his eyes, and then on the fourth morning he looked about him and said to the man beside the bed 'Hello, Doc.'

'Thank God,' breathed Hight. 'You've come through.'

It was just ten days since the events which had culminated in Sudden's being brought, unconscious, to the Lazy H ranch. Now the puncher sat in a comfortable chair and listened to the excited Billy Hornby relate the events which had taken place since the end of the siege. Doc Hight, his arm around the shoulder of Jenny Hornby, smiled indulgently as Billy told his friend his news.

153

'Yu see, the Cottons was makin' a last bid to hold on to the town, an' we never knowed it,' Billy said. 'If yu hadn't o' happened along when yu did, they'd've done it.'

'I still don't get it,' smiled Sudden. 'Why was it so important to them to keep the town under their heels?'

Hight leaned forward. 'That's the most fantastic part of the whole story, Jim,' he said. 'Shortly after yu – shortly after we got the town back to somethin' like normal, this gent turns up askin' for Fred Mott, the banker.'

'Who'd skedaddled out o' town when he seen how things was goin',' interposed Billy. 'He musta' been scared – he never even took his clothes.'

'Luckily for the town, the vault was on a time lock and couldn't be opened. Our savings, at least, are safe,' smiled Hight. 'But I was telling you: the man turned out to be a Mr Sandberg, an Inspector of Land from the territorial Legislature. He seemed astonished that we didn't know about the Government's plans to build a dam at Twin Peaks – that's not far from here, up in the hills at the end of the valley.'

'We told him somethin' about what had been goin' on,' Billy continued the story. 'He said he'd met Sim Cotton. The way he said it made it sound like he'd spotted Sim for what he was.'

'And now, dear Jim, thanks to you everyone in the valley will share in the future,' Jenny Hornby told him. 'Every acre of scrubland will be irrigated, and the whole valley will be rich, fertile land.'

'Worth a fortune,' added Hight. 'Which explains why Sim Cotton wanted to keep the town under his thumb. As soon as the dam was given the go-ahead, he'd buy up every building, every acre of land – everything would have been in his hands.'

'Until yu happened along,' Billy finished. And then, with a quizzical frown. 'Or *did* yu just happen along?'

Sudden regarded his young friend with a level gaze.

'How d'yu come to think somethin' like that?' he asked. His voice was lazy, but Hight detected something in it which Billy did not.

'Hell, Jim, I dunno,' foundered the boy. 'It was . . . just, well, as if someone'd known what was goin' on here, an' had sent yu to come an' put an end to it.'

'Shore,' scoffed Sudden. 'Someone who knowed I'd get here on the day that he knowed yu was goin' to make a play against Buck Cotton. Someone who knowed I'd be able to handle Sim Cotton an' all his boys, an' knowed that if they nearly burned me to a cinder in a blazin' stable, it'd be okay, because I'd get out an' then not get beefed, on'y creased. Shore,' he finished, 'someone sent me, I reckon. Ol' Lady Luck, kid. Nobody else.'

'Well, anyway,' Billy argued. 'It makes no never-mind – it shore was a good thing for this town that yu happened along. The Cottons was aimin' to eat this valley whole.'

'They nearly made it,' Sudden reminded him quietly.

'Aw, shucks, Jim,' protested Billy, 'they had no chance agin' yu. I never seen anythin' like that fight in the street. Three o' them, an' one o' them Sim Cotton, an' yu—'

'Was within one millimeter of cashin' in my chips,' Sudden said grimly. 'If Doc here hadn't turned up – an' I ain't yet had a chance o' thankin' yu, Doc – by the way, just where in Hades *did* yu come from?'

'From my own house,' smiled Hight. 'I woke up lying on the floor, stiff as a board from the beating Art Cotton had given me. I was surprised to find myself still alive, and astonished when I discovered I was able to walk. I found a bottle of whiskey and took a drink of that, which helped. Then I looked through the window. It all came flooding back, the fight, the siege. I could see the stable all but burned down. I could see men in the street. I imagined that yu and Billy must both be dead, and I went out to find out what had gone on. I must have not been thinking too clearly for it never occurred to me that the Cottons would kill me knowing that I'd been with yu. But then I saw you, and Buck Cotton ready to kill you. I didn't know what to do but I just kept walking, automatically, I suppose. I saw Billy's gun laying there in the dust. I didn't know really what was happening, but I was terribly tired and suddenly very angry, impatient almost, and I just threw a shot at Buck. To my surprise, it disarmed him. I thought he had already shot you, you see: you looked dead on your feet.'

'It'd been a hard sort o' day,' admitted Sudden with a smile.

'An' then the Doc yells out that if they want it to be their town, them watchin' had better do somethin' about it,' Billy interposed. 'The crowd tore Buck Cotton to pieces.'

Jenny Hornby shuddered. 'It must have been awful,' she shivered. 'Even though they were so hateful, I could not wish such a death on any man.'

'No, it wasn't pretty,' Hight agreed, 'but it was necessary. If this town was ever going to have any self-respect again.'

'I remember the crowd yelled,' Sudden told them. 'What happened after that? I must'a' been dozin' at the time.'

'Yu shore were,' chortled Billy. 'Sleepin' Beauty had nothin' on yu.'

'They found Martin Kilpatrick in the jailhouse,' Hight told his listeners. 'The townspeople wanted to hang him, but in the end he was stripped, tied to a horse, and pointed north. He left the town without a single possession.'

'At that, he was lucky,' growled Billy.

'That's true,' agreed the doctor. 'But they all agreed that Kilpatrick had been nothing but a tool.'

'Hah, listen to him!' snorted Billy. ' "They agreed", he says, as if it had been some kind of sewin' circle discussion. Jim, Doc stood over that shiverin' ol' misfit with a cocked gun in his hand, an' told that lynch mob the killin' was over – unless someone tried to lay a hand on Kilpatrick. They took his word for it, an' backed off.'

During this recital, Jenny Hornby regarded the medico with adoring eyes, while that worthy flushed crimson and fidgeted in his seat. Unable to contain his embarrassment he protested: 'Those men were only looking for a scapegoat. By hanging Kilpatrick they would be hanging their own guilt, their own refusal to fight the Cottons until it was almost too late.'

Sudden shook his head. 'That psychology stuff's too deep for me, Doc. But I'll take yore word for it. What happens now?'

'We've elected a council,' Hight told him. 'Land in the valley will be allocated to everyone in the town according to how long they've lived here. After that, new settlers will be entitled to file on the usual hundred and sixty acres allowed by the Homestead Act. For the time being, I'm acting as Mayor. And in that office, I want to tell you that we all felt that as soon as you were on your feet properly, we'd offer you the job of town Marshal, Jim.'

'Yu don't need me,' he murmured. 'The town is free.'

'It'll still be wide open for a while,' persisted Hight, 'as the new settlers come in. We'll need help, Jim. And later . . . well, you could hang up your guns for good.'

Sudden smiled sadly. It was a tempting offer, indeed, to a lonely man.

To put behind him the empty outlaw trails, the long and endless quest upon which he had embarked, to live in a friendly town, with good people for neighbours. But it could not be, and he knew it.

'If I'd lost my memory for good, it mighta been possible,' he told them. 'But now, I can't. I got a job to do.'

Hight smiled and did not press Sudden further. He dissolved Billy's puzzled frown by saying 'We'll manage. I have another man who I think will handle the job admirably – Billy, here.'

'Me?' ejaculated the boy. 'Town Marshal? An' who's goin' to look after the Lazy H?' He looked at his sister who smiled at him slowly and then looked towards the doctor. Billy finally grinned. 'Oh, I see,' he nodded. 'It looks like Town Marshal or workin' for Doc an' Jenny. In which case—'

'Yu'll take it, I suppose?' finished Hight, joining in the general laugher at Billy's predicament. Jenny turned again to Sudden.

'And you, Jim? Won't you stay awhile with us – at least for the wedding?'

'I'd admire to,' Green told her. 'But I oughta be moseyin' on, soon as Doc tells me I can ride.'

'Oh, David, tell him he can't ride until after the wedding,' pouted Jenny Hornby, charmingly.

'I don't imagine he'd believe me, somehow,' replied Hight. 'He probably knows as well as I do that he could be in the saddle a couple of days from now. The loss of memory was

157

purely temporary, and Jim's as healthy as a horse. I don't think I could fool him – but I'm still hoping he'll stay.'

But in the end, their arguments availed them nothing, and they reluctantly realised that their friend was going to leave them. They had one final surprise left for him, however, which Jenny whispered to him that evening as they had supper.

'They're doin' what?' he asked, amazed.

'It's true,' Jim,' she dimpled. 'Ask David.'

'Consider yoreself asked, Doc,' Sudden said. 'What's this about changin' the name o' the town?'

'Oh, it was just an idea we had,' Hight said airily. Billy stifled a giggle.

'Come on, Doc – give!' growled the puncher threateningly, and Hight smiled.

'They want to call the town Green Valley, Jim – if it's okay with you. As a permanent reminder to those who were here of what happened.'

Sudden's face was unreadable, his friends looked puzzled.

'You don't like it?' queried Billy, anxiously.

Sudden's voice, when he finally spoke, was husky with emotion. 'It's a fine thought, Doc. But . . . yu ought to name it for Davis, mebbe, or Blass. They belonged here. They gave their lives for this town. Me, I was just ridin' through, like that Ishmael fella in the Bible – a born drifter. Not the kind o' jasper to name yore town after.'

'I'll tell the council,' Hight said, finally. 'But I'm thinking they won't change their minds.'

'Talking of changing minds, have you changed yours, Jim?' asked Jenny Hornby. 'You promised to think about staying for the wedding.'

Sudden shook his head. 'The doctor says I can ride in a couple o' days, Jenny. I reckon I'll mosey.'

'This town will find it mighty hard to part with you,' Hight told him. Sudden shook his head.

'Nobody's indispensable,' he said, and Hight thought he detected sadness in the voice. He mentioned the fact later, as he and Sudden sat on the porch smoking a last cigarette before turning in. Inside the house, Jenny could be heard squealing as her brother splashed water at her during the chore of dishwashing.

'I hate to see you go, Jim,' Hight ventured. 'Are you sure . . . ?'

'Leave it alone, now, Doc,' Sudden said quietly. 'I'm shore.'

'Hell, Jim, you may never find those two men you're looking for!' snorted Hight, disgustedly.

'Not if I wait for 'em to come to me, Doc.' Then his voice dropped. 'Yu ain't told Billy – about me?'

Hight shook his head. 'Never a word. Why?'

'Don't yu. Not for a long, long time. Mebbe if yu ever hear I've done what I've set out to do, tell him then.'

Many years later, when the news finally reached the sheltered valley that Sudden's quest was indeed over, Hight was to recall their quiet conversation, sitting on the darkened porch, beneath the brilliant stars.

'You want to tell me why the boy shouldn't know, Jim?'

'Shucks, that's easy, Doc. If he was to hear some o' the tales that are told about Sudden, he might just want to defend me – in my absence, like. It ain't worth it.'

'Jim, your thinking does you credit,' Hight told him, 'but you sell yoreself short. Why, I'd be proud to stand up and tell the world I know you.'

Sudden's smile was wry. 'Well . . . don't do it in Texas,' was all he said.

A few days later, the three men rode into town, gathering for their final farewell on the porch of Hight's little house. The busy sound of hammering, and the yells of working men came from the skeleton frame of a new stable, being built upon the cleared site of the charred ruin.

'When she's finished, nobody'll know that any o' this ever happened,' Billy Hornby remarked almost petulantly.

'Just as well, that way,' Sudden replied. 'The town's had its operation. Now the scar's healin'. The sooner folks forget the Cottons, the better the place'll be.' He thrust out his hand, the other on the boy's shoulder.

'So long, Billy,' he said, gruffly. 'An' don't pick any more fights until I'm long gone, yu hear?'

'So long, Jim,' muttered Billy. He could not, finally, meet the level eyes of his friend without revealing the tears lurking in his own. Billy watched as the medico and his protector clasped hands, neither speaking. Then Sudden mounted the big black, the magnificent stallion impatient to set out on the open road after his enforced idleness. Sudden looked down at his good friends.

'Green Valley, huh?' he grinned. 'Shore is a hell of a name to give a town.'

He lifted a hand in final farewell and turned the horse towards the north. They watched him thunder up the street, and within moments the curve hid him from their view. Before them lay the everyday bustle of the town, with people going about their business in complete normality. Hight nodded to himself.

Had 'Green' been sent to help them? Was it possible that the infamous gunfighter Sudden was perhaps some kind of undercover trouble-shooter? Nonsense, he told himself. He turned to find Billy frowning at him.

'I was just wonderin' about what Jim said, Doc,' Billy started. 'Yu reckon he was agreein' to us callin' the town Green Valley or not? Like he said: It's kind o' out o' the ordinary, ain't it?'

Hight nodded in agreement.

'You're right, Billy,' he told the youngster. 'But the name stays. It's out of the ordinary, all right – but so is the man we're namin' it after.'